D1580017

C0000 002 405 996

THE BEACON

Fiction
Gentleman and Ladies
A Change for the Better
I'm the King of the Castle
The Albatross and Other Stories
Strange Meeting
The Bird of Night
A Bit of Singing and Dancing
In the Springtime of the Year
The Woman in Black
Mrs De Winter
The Mist in the Mirror
Air and Angels
The Service of Clouds
The Boy Who Taught the Beekeeper to Read
The Man in the Picture

Non-Fiction
The Magic Apple Tree
Family

Featuring Simon Serrailler
The Various Haunts of Men
The Pure in Heart
The Risk of Darkness
The Vows of Silence

Children's Books
The Battle for Gullywith

The Beacon

Susan Hill

Chatto & Windus

LONDON

Published by Chatto & Windus 2008

2 4 6 8 10 9 7 5 3 1

Copyright © Susan Hill 2008

Susan Hill has asserted her right under the Copyright, Designs and
Patents Act 1988 to be identified as the author of this work

First published in Great Britain in 2008 by
Chatto & Windus
Random House, 20 Vauxhall Bridge Road,
London SW1V 2SA

www.rbooks.co.uk

Addresses for companies within The Random House Group
Limited can be found at: www.randomhouse.co.uk/offices.htm

The Random House Group Limited Reg. No. 954009

A CIP catalogue record for this book
is available from the British Library

ISBN 9780701183400

The Random House Group Limited makes every effort to ensure
that the papers used in its books are made from trees that have been
legally sourced from well-managed and credibly certified forests.
Our paper procurement policy can be found at:
www.randomhouse.co.uk/paper.htm

I

May Prime had been with her mother all after-noon, sitting in the cane chair a few feet away from the bed, but suddenly at seven o'clock she had jumped up and run out of the house and into the yard and stood staring at the gathering sky because she could not bear the dying a second longer.

And when she returned only a little later Bertha was dead. May knew it had happened as she walked back into the house, before reaching the bedroom, before seeing her. She knew it from the change in everything and from the silence. But she still drew in her breath and her hand went to her mouth when she looked down.

The farmhouse was called the Beacon and they had been born and reared there, Colin, Frank, May and

1

Berenice, but only May had been left for the last twenty-seven years to live with both their parents and then, after their father's death, with their mother alone.

One week, their father had been helping to haul a cow out of a ditch and, the next, most of the animals had gone. Bertha Prime had called in a neighbour and had them sent to market. Only the chickens had remained.

After that, Bertha had let out the fields. Otherwise life had stayed the same. There were no animals to feed and milk early and late and, once Frank moved out, no man to do it anyway.

It was no longer usual, in the 1960s, for an unmarried girl to go on living with her parents, their insurance against the deprivations of old age, and if they had ever been asked about it directly, John and, after John, Bertha would have said that they would be more than happy for May to leave home, preferably to be married but if not that then for a career. They had neither asked nor expected her to remain with them. It had just happened.

May would have said the same. It had just happened. 'Fallen out that way.' There was more to it than that, of course, but John and Bertha did not know the 'more' and May preferred to bury it.

Perhaps Bertha guessed something but if she did she never spoke of it.

She stood in the doorway, hand to mouth, and her mother lay in the bed with the slatted oak frame and she was dead. From that moment everything was different. She was a dead body, not Bertha, not her mother.

May had been with her, watching from the front porch, when they had brought her dead father home and carried him up and laid him down on this same bed, so she knew the appearance of death, as she recognised the absoluteness of the silence. But it was shocking all the same. She went unsteadily across the room and sat in the cane chair, but for several minutes could not look at the bed.

2

J OHN AND Bertha Prime had taken the Beacon over from John's father and mother, and had moved in as one family in the last years of the thirties, and to Bertha living with them was what she had expected and the hard work was expected too. She had not come from a farming family – her parents had kept the village store – but no one could have lived at the Beacon without understanding what the life of everyone around them entailed. Only the large landowners had cottages into which sons and their new families could sometimes move. John Prime's father, also John Prime, was no such man.

John and Bertha had come back from their wedding straight to the attic bedroom, which had been turned out and cleaned in their honour, with new curtains and a new mattress for the old bed but nothing else, and the following morning Bertha had come downstairs to work in the dairy with her new mother-in-law. After the dairy there were the chickens and then the geese, and after the geese the beehives, and after that the kitchen, and that was life at the Beacon. Once a week she spent an afternoon with her own parents and served in the store, and at first it felt as if she had never left but, before long, this was changed and that was changed, things were in a new place, the shelving was rearranged, and Bertha had soon felt like a stranger who knew nothing of the way things should be.

They were married in July and in November she stopped going to the store every week and when she did go, she no longer served there because she got in the way and slowed things down, they said, and besides, now she was pregnant with her first child.

The baby, a boy, was born on the hottest day of the following summer while every available man and woman was out in the fields and Bertha lay and sweated in the attic bedroom through thirteen hours of labour. John Prime lived for half an hour only, and the next summer another baby was stillborn, though this one came in the night of torrential rain that washed a ton of mud and stones down the hill and half a flock of sheep were buried.

Her mother-in-law was not unfeeling, not unkind,

but having lost three children of her own, accepted those things as inevitable and said very little, though she did not press Bertha to return to the dairy or the kitchen, but let her work things out in her own time. But sitting alone in the attic or going for silent walks along the lanes and through the fields near the Beacon gave her thoughts of death, and when her mind turned twice to drowning and she caught herself looking at the strong branch of a tree, Bertha went back at once to work in the dairy and among the chickens, terrified.

Her husband, John, was sympathetic but uncomfortable and in any case spent little time with her, because there was always too much work to be done and that was the way of it. Only sometimes in winter, when the weather was bad and the nights drawn in, he would come with his father to sit beside the fire next to her and drink a glass of ale and talk a little, though always about the farm or the state of the land or the prices at market. Once or twice they would listen to the wireless and afterwards talk would turn to the wider world and what would happen if there was another war, as seemed likely. But the talk was brief and petered out with the dying fire and then it was time for the women to set out the bread and cheese and last drinks before bed.

Two days before the outbreak of war, Bertha went

into a short, sharp labour with Colin, who was nine pounds of furious health, and barely a year later Frank was born and a family was established and no one looked back, though Bertha went to the churchyard every Easter and Christmas to put flowers on the infant graves. In the years when she had been ill and first housebound and then bedridden, May had taken over the duty, because she was asked and because it was something that had just always been done like so much else in a life filled with habit and custom and a small amount of ritual.

May herself arrived in the spring of 1942, born in the same bedroom but only just, for by now Bertha's labours were even quicker and the baby had almost been born in the kitchen and then on the last treads of the stairs.

May was neither large nor robust but a long, pale, straggling baby who would not suckle and seemed to have no appetite for life. In the end, it was her grandmother who coaxed her forward a little further each day when Bertha's milk had run out, by giving the baby milk fresh from the cow and sitting patiently with her on a kitchen stool until she had finished a bottle. The two boys thrived and raced about.

Because their lives were already hard, the war brought nothing very much worse, and indeed, in some ways it was easier because it brought extra help on all the farms, in the shape of prisoners of war and even land girls, though the latter were never sent to the Beacon. The Prime family were better off for food than many others – the men shot rabbits and there were always fruit and mushrooms for those who knew where to look.

May was three when her grandfather died and she remembered nothing of him but the smell of his tobacco which seemed to come from the pores of his skin and the hair of his head and be woven like another layer of thread into every item of his clothing. When he died, John Prime moved into his shoes and the only difference was that now he gave instead of took the orders. The work was just the same. But there was never any question of John and Bertha moving out of the attic down to the big bedroom and the large bed. If the widow had ever felt it was her place to give them up now to the next generation, as others would and had in her position, she said nothing and did nothing and so everything remained as it had and Bertha could not ask. It was another ten years before Bertha attained the large room and the biggest bed, and by then she had forgotten that they had once been so prized. The attic was hers. The attic was where her marriage had begun, the attic was her marriage's own private space, her small world, and in the end she was reluctant to leave it. But by then Colin and Frank needed a bigger room and May moved into theirs, and so everything changed and life went on with only a pause for the shifting of mattresses.

They kept dairy cows and a few beef cattle, sheep and pigs and chickens, with geese and turkeys for Christmas, and they grew wheat and barley and potatoes, and as the land was partly on the side of the hill that stretched away from the Beacon and partly on the plain running down to the river, the work was both varied and never-ending. After the war they stopped using horses and bought a tractor and the milking gradually became more mechanised, but that did not shrink the working hours and the weather was against them for seven months of the year in this distant and uphill place.

May had fragmented memories of growing up at the Beacon, like a series of pictures in an album except that sometimes the pictures had sound or came with their own smell and taste. Someone from the village brought a grandchild of the same age, Sylvia, and Sylvia and May had wandered out into the strawberry patch and eaten the fruit warm from the sun until their mouths were scarlet and their stomachs ached. The taste and the smell of the berries and the straw they rested in and the earth beneath it were there for the taking for the rest of May's life if she read or heard the single word 'strawberry'.

The pain in the back of her legs after climbing the hill and the feel of the rain and wind stinging her face.

Her grandmother's smell when she was old. May had not liked to go near her in the chair or in her bed because of the smell which was of something both decaying and oddly sweet.

She had gone to school on the bus from the end of the track, but memories of school were even more fragmented. The feel of a wooden ruler in her hand and, once, being told that a girl in her class had measles very badly, and then next, that she was dead.

The shiny green tiles in the washroom. The cold water that made your teeth ache when you drank it from the tap, cupping your hand and filling it first then scooping the hand to your mouth.

But there were no really bad memories and that was important. Later, when she had to sit down and go step by step through her life – their lives – from far back to the present, she could not conjure up anything that was more than a passing unpleasantness that went with everyone's childhood – pain in a tooth or a boil or disappointment over something postponed. Life had simply gone on uneventfully until, when she was six, her sister and the last child had been born and christened Berenice. Sheila had been their grand-mother's chosen name; John Prime would have gone along with anything. No one quite knew where Bertha had found the name Berenice.

From the beginning, May had loved her with a protective and slavish intensity, spending every moment she could hanging over the cot and the pram, answering her cries with an urgency that everyone said would be regretted. The baby had seemed complacent and self-absorbed and as she grew up had taken her sister's attentiveness so much for granted that it had warped her character. But May had con-tinued to love and serve, and secretly, Bertha had found it a relief not to have more work, more calls on her attention. She had realised very quickly that the baby could be left to May.

May Prime was clever. That had been clear when she had picked out letters on the back of her father's newspaper as he held it up and then found the same letters in the family Bible and in the stock book and in the books from the glass case in the sitting room. She had found pencil and paper and copied the groups of letters until they formed words and asked for the words to be read and whispered them over and over, staring at the marks until they gave up their secret to her and she could read. That had been before she went to school and was a thing unheard of in the family, though both her grandmother and Bertha Prime read books during the winter and her father went through the paper from front to back every day after dinner.

She had loved to read and later to take the arithmetic books from her brothers and try to work out the exercises, though numbers did not make the same sense to her that words did. There was a globe of the world in the front room, beside the single glass-fronted case of books – Shakespeare, Sir Walter Scott, an encyclopedia, a dictionary, *Everyman in Health and Sickness*, the prayer book, *The Ready Reckoner*. She sometimes took down the globe and twirled it on its stand and read the names of the countries aloud.

By the time she went to school with Colin and Frank she could read and had an odd, random confetti in her brain of bits of knowledge which floated about and changed shape like the tiny shards of bright glass inside her brother's kaleidoscope. In the end the fragments would come together in a linear form, though some would prove incorrect or useless and others were lost altogether.

She loved the school from the first moment of walking into the cloakroom and finding her own name on a piece of card slotted into a little metal holder above a peg. Her name. She loved the smell of the entrance and the different, wood-dust smell of the hall and the smell of the classrooms which were placed all around it, a different smell again, of chalk dust and of other children.

She fell into schoolwork. She loved the exercise books she was given, one of which had times tables, rules and measures on the back, the other lists of the principal rivers and mountains of the world, of Kings and Queens, of Important Dates and Capital Cities and the Constellations. She learned them by heart without trying because she looked at them so often, read them so many times, that her mind, almost her skin, simply absorbed them.

As she moved up from class to class everything became more interesting and the exercise books now had algebraic and chemical formulae and French and Latin verbs. The beginning of each term, when she wrote her name on each book, filled her with a huge excitement for the knowledge that was waiting for her, the exercises to come.

Yet she was a friendly girl too; she learned skipping games and five stones and catching rhymes and huddled against the wall hearing tales. She played rounders because she had an excellent ball eye, though her running was awkward. She could jump higher than any other girl in the school and played the recorder well enough to be in the band.

When she was seven she acquired a particular friend who had come to the school that term.

Patricia Hogg's father was the new gamekeeper to the big estate on the other side of the hill, across the valley from the Beacon, and for a time, May, Patricia Hogg and a girl called Geraldine were always closeted together. But, three being a crowd, Geraldine was edged out, and May and Patricia Hogg were left to sit together, eat lunch together, walk part of the way home together. Patricia Hogg was a reader like May and in spring and summer they took their library books and sat in the sun on the wall or on the grassy bank, skirts hitched up above their knees so their legs would brown.

Patricia Hogg had none of May's fire for learning and the books she read were always school or fairy stories, but they formed a comfortable pairing.

Once, May was invited to stay with Patricia Hogg at the gamekeeper's cottage, which sent Bertha into a spasm of uncertainty and alarm, for no member of the Prime family had been to stay at the house of anyone who was not a close relative as far back as anyone could remember, so that there was the worry of what state May's clothes were in and how she should carry them and if presents ought to be taken.

But in the end this was sewn and that was mended and everything was clean and a canvas bag found in one of the upstairs trunks and a jar of honey and a slab of home-cured bacon wrapped in greaseproof and settled among the cotton knickers and white socks.

She had left with Patricia Hogg after school, walking importantly out of the gate carrying the canvas bag. They walked to the opposite end of the village from the one which led to the Beacon, and waited in the sun for a bus. When it came it was full with people coming back from the market and they had to stand, holding onto the cracked leather seat backs and swaying about as the bus went round the bends. She could remember the feel of the leather in her hand, years afterwards.

The cottage was on the very edge of the estate and backed onto the woods. It was small and dark with low ceilings and you went in straight from the street. There was no porch.

There were five of them living in the cottage with the indoors dog and two cats, and with May it was crowded and felt more so when the gamekeeper came in from work. He was a huge man. They were all huge, with large hands and feet, and Mrs Hogg had a great, wide backside which seemed to fill half the kitchen when she bent over.

May slept in the same bed as Patricia. She had never in her life slept in a bed with anyone else and crept to the far side and held onto the edge in case their legs touched. To May, sharing a bed was a strange and unpleasant thing to do, and hot, too, under the heavy quilt.

The Beacon was never completely silent because of being high up and always troubled by a wind, but here the woods seemed to press into the house like baize, so that no air could get through and the light was oddly green. She could not get to sleep for the stillness and the odd shrieks of creatures out in the darkness, and then she began to want the lavatory. She tried to ignore the pressure of it but in the end she had to whisper to Patricia, and not knowing what to say, asked, 'Has your dad locked up downstairs?'

The toilet was outside at the bottom of the thin garden close to the trees.

'Why, what are you frightened of?'

'I'm not frightened. I need to go to the toilet.'

'There's something under the bed for that.'

May had been mortified. There were pots under the beds at home too, though also a proper flush toilet in a lean-to beyond the scullery. The idea of using a pot with someone else in the room, even in the dark, was quite shocking. She lay absolutely still on the far edge of the bed and in spite of the discomfort eventually slept. She woke sometime later. It was still pitch black, and Patricia was making tiny snorting sounds. May slid inch by inch from the bed onto the floor and then felt around for the pot on the rough boards, praying for the other girl not to wake.

In some ways everything at the Hoggs' cottage was familiar. The dark. The fact that the outside world seemed to be inside too, the sounds the pigs made and the smells. Otherwise, it was entirely strange, denser and closer, as if everyone and everything was packed tightly together, bodies and clothes, china and pans, cats and chairs and the gamekeeper's guns and sticks.

There were the indoor dog, and two cats, but no animals other than two pigs and the gun dogs which lived in outside cages and the ferrets, and the wood came right to the fence and one day might have marched into the house like a wood in a fairy story.

May learned an early lesson about people, which is that they can change according to their settings and how they fit into them. Patricia Hogg at home was not the same as the one she knew at school. At home she took the lead and was not always friendly, sulked and was cocky. She was the eldest child of three and the only girl.

They went for desultory walks and sat in the fringes of the wood among leaves and pine needles with their backs against the tree trunks. May had brought a book but Patricia did not want to read. She did not seem to want her here and there was nothing to talk about.

They had been shooed out of the house after breakfast.

It was a dismal three days and May felt that she was doing wrong simply by being her usual self, but she had no other self to present and found herself, for the first but not the last time, without resources and unable to mould herself to blend with her surroundings or to fit in with the expectations of others. She had no idea what those expectations were. The difference in the other girl was both a shock and a puzzle and she did not know how to relate to this new Patricia Hogg.

She finished her book and asked if she could borrow another but there was only the Bible in the cottage, so she found herself reading Exodus and Isaiah and Revelation by the light of the oil lamp at the kitchen table while they drank beakers of cocoa and Mrs Hogg banged the iron down onto sheets and shirts. Always after, that biblical language was associated for May with the smell of the hot flannel and the dusty taste of cocoa so that wafts of one or the other came to her if she was in church or heard the Bible being read aloud anywhere.

The weekend with Patricia Hogg taught her so much that she was still absorbing the lessons months later. She learned about how differently others live and speak to one another, that friends can be slippery and friendships treacherous and that you needed to have resources within yourself to make up for it.

Inevitably, her friendship with Patricia changed and they spent less time together, and when the question of her coming in turn to the Beacon was raised, May was at first evasive and later, when it recurred, said that Patricia was afraid of sleeping in strange houses. She knew that her mother was quietly relieved. There was enough to do and more without the anxiety of having a visitor.

During May's last years at the village school her friendships were more numerous and also more casual, and in any case she was focusing on the scholarship to the grammar school which would take her away from many of the people she had been with from the beginning. She longed for the senior school, longed for the new lessons and the new books, the uniform and the opening out of world upon world. It was taken for granted that she would pass the examination and so she believed it and made plans in her mind accordingly. The others would go to the secondary school in the market town; the grammar was fifteen miles and a much longer bus ride away. During the final term and after the exam, May detached herself from the village school and everyone in it little by little, though no one else was aware of it.

She did so instinctively and to harden herself, not wanting to be hurt by the pain of the final separation. It was the place she would miss and the loss of it would affect her no matter where she went next, for the small building was what she had loved the most, and although she was eager for her future and the new life, she did not yet know what the new school was like or how strong an attachment she might develop for it.

At home, nothing changed outwardly but Berenice grew and in growing she too began to reveal herself. She was a spoilt and manipulative child, prone to tears and tantrums and to sudden fevers which gave her fits and caused terror in everyone other than May, who had a calm inner knowledge that Berenice would always survive. No mere physical illness, no fever however high and dramatic would ever get the better of her – that much was perfectly clear to May, though to May alone. And yet May loved her as much now that her true nature was visible as she had when Berenice had been a quiet and undemanding baby, and Berenice accepted her sister's attentions and love as her due and was nourished and enriched by it.

May loved her brother Colin because he was so easy, so straightforward, so readable and predictable. Life for Colin was an uncomplicated business because it was entirely outward. He had, apparently, no inner life whatsoever, no private thoughts or concealed feelings, no complex responses to other people or to events. Life was linear. Colin had no favourites and no secrets, he treated everyone according to their status in the hierarchy, looked to himself, was generous and hard-working and ended every day in every way the same as he had begun it.

And then there was Frank.

3

AFTER A time she went up to the bed and looked down at her mother's dead body. Her eyes were open but they were not 'her' eyes now, they were 'the' eyes. Already the body had become impersonal.

Tentatively, May reached out her hand. She should close the eyes. The sightless blank stare was more frightening than anything else, but she had never done such a thing, though read of it often enough, and did not know if the eyelids would yield. But when she pressed gently on the soft, tender tissue and moved it forward, it slid down over the eyeball quite easily.

The head lay light on the pillow. She had become a light thing of bones and skin and hair over the last few months, flesh had dissolved and withered away and she weighed almost nothing; there was scarcely any impression on the mattress.

The room was thick with the silence. May felt that it stuffed her lungs with something dry and cloth-like as she breathed it in instead of air. The silence went through the whole house, like smoke from the hearth.

She did not know what she should do next. She had not prepared for this moment, though it had been coming for long enough. Somehow she had expected it to happen earlier in the day when other people might be here, even if the Beacon was never full of people as it used to be; mostly she was here with Bertha alone.

A tiny spider was on the back of the dead hand, quite still, and it occurred to her that the hand would not feel the tickling of the insect now. The hand felt nothing.

She turned away. She went from the bedroom and down the stairs and out of the house altogether, suddenly desperate for air, and stood in the dark gulping it in as she might gulp water in great thirst. And it was air, cool, fresh, with the taste of the hill and the earth and the night upon it, and it refreshed her. She looked up at the sky and a picture on the back of one of her exercise books with the drawing of the globe and the constellations came to her mind.

There were thin skeins of cloud winding in front of the moon. She crossed the yard.

Everything was empty, the animals long gone. She

went into the pigsties and the stables where the iron rack still had some wisps of hay and there was straw on the floor brushed up against the wall. The cattle sheds were bare and dark and cold and swept clean. The stones were loose here and there beneath her feet. The wire of the chicken shed was torn away at the bottom. She went inside. The earth was bone dry but there was still the faint sour chicken smell inside the wooden house and just visible stains of droppings on the floor.

In and out of every building, in and out, opening doors, walking around, hearing her own footsteps and nothing else, nothing else.

In the house the body of her mother lay alone and she would rather be here, remembering the warm breath of animals and the feeling of their hot rough tongues, the silken inner ears of the pigs and the coarse hairy skin of their backs, the bones of the chickens beneath the mounds of soft feather.

She walked round slowly. Since the animals went, she had scarcely been out here. The buildings were collapsing. A few winter gales and more gates would break from their hinges, more slates and stones come crashing down. The farmhouse itself was sound enough and she had kept it clean and painted. She had wondered occasionally whether they ought at least to get back some chickens and a few geese and loan out the stables for a riding horse but had never got round to it. Besides, her mother had set her face against any animals. Animals were to do with the past and the way the Beacon used to be, not this half-life she had lived for the past twenty or more years with May, shut away from the outside and whatever belonged to it. Now, May stood in the chicken shed and thought, yes, she would get some day-olds, next spring, for there was no one to stop her. She could do as she liked.

She went out into the dark of the farmyard again. The moon had slipped out of sight and a wind came whispering up the hill towards her in advance, as always, of a gale later.

Far down she saw the lights of the village and of the farm on the opposite slope. There had always been pitch black up here at night and as a child she had grown used to coming home up the black lane from the bus and having an instinctive sense of what was around and ahead of her, but gradually she had lost that sense and had to feel her way anxiously or use a torch.

She had left the light on in the porch and the hall and upstairs in the front bedroom. She looked at the house, sailing like a ship at sea, visible for so many miles around. The Beacon.

It occurred to her that no one in the universe other

than herself knew yet that Bertha was dead. It could not go on being so but for the moment, as she stood in the dark and the rising wind, it was like holding a secret to herself.

She had felt nothing after the immediate shock of finding her mother dead, nothing at all, and wondered if it would come, sadness, grief, loss, bereavement. She had lived with Bertha for so many years there must be some hurt, and before that she had been here with the others and her father too, never, ever completely alone.

The only time she had been separated from the Beacon and the people of it had been the year she had spent in London, and that she could barely remember, it was so long ago and a life so wholly other, so detached from everything in her experience before or after. Very occasionally, shards of memory of that time came to her like very faded scents and sounds, and usually she could not find a reason for their reappearance, no reminder, no link from present to past, they were simply there, briefly, as she did some job, sat here or there.

She was conscious of the minutes passing, moving her away from the time when her mother had been alive and from the moment when she had found her dead and moving her forwards to whatever she had to do. She realised that she did not quite know. There seemed no urgency. The body in the bed needed nothing. She needed nothing. What was there to do?

She looked back up at the night sky, huge and impersonal. Smelled the air which had grown colder as she had been out.

Was it the doctor she had to call? The undertaker? Which undertaker? The silence in the house would be broken by people entering it. The time when it was May and the dead body of her mother would be over and she would have to open her arms to the time that was coming when everything would change.

But it has already changed, she thought. It has changed now. Better get on with things then. Ringing the doctor. Ringing the undertaker.

And then the others.

Colin. Berenice.

Frank. He ought to be told. He had the right to know. But she would not tell him and she doubted if the others would bring themselves to speak to him either.

4

THE YEARS at the grammar school, to which she had indeed won a scholarship, were, she knew now, the best of her life because every day she looked forward, every day she was a step further into the future, which she knew, as everyone knew, was to be entirely successful and a fulfilment. She did not know in which direction she might go, though it was not likely to have much to do with maths and science at which she had to work harder than others to keep pace. Languages were possible. History she found endlessly interesting, and her childhood delight in the globe she had spun round with her finger never left her, so that geography was something she always looked forward to. She liked reading the English set books, the poems and the novels, though not the plays because she found anything theatrical and dramatic embarrassing. She was an orderly girl, her desk always tidy, her work always marked high for neatness. Early on one of her teachers told her she should think of the Civil Service because she would run an office so efficiently. She wondered about teaching history. She would go somewhere, take up something, fulfil her promise. It was not that she longed to escape the Beacon. She was happy there. Home was home and a familiar comfort, and there were times as she grew up when the idea of leaving it to study or work in some distant place filled her with fear but also seemed so unlikely that she gave it little thought.

She made a great many friends but none of them was ever close and she never again went to stay at someone else's house, though there were plenty of visits to dinner and tea and those girls occasionally came to the Beacon.

One, Janet Fairley, was quite new, having come to live in the village only the year before from some-where much farther north. Her father ran the garage, selling petrol and servicing the farm vehicles and the private cars that more people were now acquiring. Her mother had a couple of rooms in the house which she let whenever they were needed.

Janet Fairley was a bright-faced, open-hearted girl who had brought novelty to a class of girls who knew one another too well and had grown bored. She was friendly towards everyone, made no enemies and joined in no quarrels. And when May had asked her to tea at the Beacon her brother Colin had first talked to her more than he ever talked to anyone and then taken her round the farm, explaining the animals and the machines and the way of everything, earnestly and carefully, as if it were important for her to know and understand everything. May had been taken aback at the way her friend had been appropriated. Her mother had watched him with nervous eyes.

The following Saturday evening, Colin had brushed his hair back and glued it down with water and polished his shoes and walked into the village. Later, they learned that he had called at the Fairley house. The week after that he had taken Janet on the bus into town. They had gone to the pictures.

A year later, Janet Fairley's mother had died very suddenly and Janet had left school and taken over both the running of the house and the paperwork of the garage. A year after that Colin had married her, and then Arthur Fairley had met a woman in town who, within a couple of months, was his own new wife.

It was not Colin's marriage which caused the grief in the family, it was his announcement that he was not staying at the Beacon but going to work as a stockman on a farm the other side of the valley. John Prime had sat silent in the kitchen night after night, arms folded on the table in front of him, bewildered, uncertain who or what to blame.

But after Colin and Janet Fairley were married, and Colin had left, a new farmhand came to help and things rolled on much as before, though there was more room to move in the house. They could spread themselves comfortably around the kitchen table.

Berenice passed for the grammar school, though she did not get a scholarship which meant that money was tighter. May had dreaded her being there for all that she loved her sister, but Berenice kept her distance, and did not acknowledge her during school hours, and put everyone she met under her thumb. She was clever and lazy and had a winning smile which kept her in everyone's favour and May was left to get on, purposefully working towards her future.

During this time Frank was almost invisible. Frank had done everything late – walked, talked, and as he grew older he talked less than any of them. He spent a lot of time alone, wandering about the farm, sitting under hedgerows and in the hayfield, apparently doing nothing. He was towards the bottom of his class at the village school and he seemed to bewilder the teachers, the other children and his parents most of all. They never knew what to make of Frank, they said; no one knew what Frank was thinking; what went on in Frank's head was one of the great mysteries. He grew taller than the others, though he never appeared to eat a full meal, and he was unnervingly thin, his head apparently sprouting from the bony cavity of his neck and shoulders as if from a coat hanger. He did little speaking but a great deal of staring out of large green-grey, slightly bulbous eyes. He followed people too, his father and the men about the farm, his mother in the house, the other children at school almost anywhere. Turn round and Frank would be there, silent, watching, following.

The one he liked best in the family was Berenice. They sometimes spent an hour or more closeted together whispering. But as Berenice grew up she eased herself away from him and he drifted off to spend more time alone. May neither knew nor understood him because there seemed little to take and keep hold of for more than a few minutes, as Frank slipped and slithered out of her ken. She subscribed to the general opinion: what goes on in Frank's head is a mystery.

He liked the animals and helped sometimes with milking and feeding, but John Prime seemed to have no confidence that he would be able to take on more of the work and eventually the whole farm, even if he showed signs of wanting to do so. He showed no signs of having interest or talent in any direction, though he was never rude, never wilful, and May often suspected that he was their mother's favourite. She had caught them in the kitchen, Frank being given some small treat or simply special attention.

But for the most part Frank, like Berenice, slipped almost out of May's sight.

She narrowed down her special subjects gradually, dropping maths and sciences and, reluctantly, deciding on history rather than geography. She excelled in French and English and it was decided that she would try for a university place and a county scholarship, for without funding there would be no question of her being able to go. John and Bertha Prime looked at her bemusedly, proud, puzzled and a little nervous, wondering if a clever child who went away to educate herself further and presumably to make a life elsewhere was what they had ever intended.

It occurred to Bertha that there were very few careers open to a woman but that teaching was the most obvious. Having had the thought, she allowed it to become a hope and then an assumption. It was the way she dealt with many of the things in life which she did not control. From then on, in her own mind, May was going to study to become a teacher and, once trained, would naturally return home. There were schools, and teachers would always be needed. Once she had settled her daughter's course for life she was quite happy. She told her husband what was likely to happen to May and he saw no reason to argue. May, as a teacher, would fit back into the family perfectly well.

Teaching was not what May had in mind. She liked school but the idea of going back to one, even in another capacity, filled her with dread, for that would be going back not moving forward and May wanted change and new challenges, other worlds.

Colin and Janet had their first child, called Eve, the year after they were married and another daughter quickly after that and so were entirely caught up, as John and Bertha had been before them, in the life of a farm and a family. The only difference, as Bertha often mentioned, was that they had their own place and the luxury of not having to share it with an older generation; they made their own choices, worked for themselves, enjoyed a more prosperous way.

But it was understood that in due course Colin would return to take over the Beacon and bring his family to live there again. No one spoke of it, no one asked, it was just the way of things.

May had worked steadily, done well in her exams, got the scholarship, sailing through it all in a state of extraordinary calm. She had applied to two universities within an hour of home, and also to London, where she had never been and which was a five-hour train journey away.

She was invited to an interview.

There was a way to do these things, the headmistress said, and a way not to do them and if you did them the correct way you had every chance of making a good impression but if you did them the wrong way, however clever you were, however good your results, you would make a poor impression and be marked down.

The way to make the right impression, those who had been given an interview were told, sitting in a nervous group together, was to wear a hat and gloves. The hat should be small and plain, the gloves should be leather and dark in colour. Everything else, it was implied, would follow as the night did the day.

May had one hat, a straw one bought when she was thirteen for her confirmation, and a pair of white cotton gloves.

'There's my beige felt,' Bertha said uncertainly.

'Oh, that would be far too big.'

'I do have some black leather gloves. Somewhere.'

May found them after a long search through the two bottom drawers of her mother's chest, wrapped in tissue. They had tiny pinprick holes all over the palms and buttoned at the side. May had bigger hands than her mother and could not get them on. Bertha said they could be damped and stretched and tried that evening, only to see the gloves harden and shrink even further. The wet leather smelled sour.

They had gone into town the following week, Bertha, May and Berenice, who would never miss a trip during which money might be spent on her, and found a plain chocolate beret and dark brown gloves straight away so that there was time for Berenice to try on a new coat and then to have tea in the department store, which was a thing May last remembered doing before she went to the grammar school. She liked it. She liked sitting in the mushroom-and-gold-painted room which had pillars and tall windows overlooking the square and eating a teacake. Bertha had a teacake. Berenice had an expensive ice-cream sundae in a tall glass.

'If you pass this interview I don't know what we'll do next,' Bertha said, her eyes watery, though with the heat of the tea room not with tears.

'I'll arrange it all, there's nothing for you to do.'

Bertha sighed. But May meant what she said. She would get her place and she would find out about everything and arrange it all. It was her future. There was nothing for her mother to do. Her father had once mumbled about money, but that would be arranged as well, May told him, the scholarship paid for everything. There was nothing for him to do either, and so he and Bertha watched as the future came rushing towards them and carried May away, leaving them breathless like watchers on a shore.

May organised her room in the student hostel, her clothes, transport for her luggage, books and stationery, opened a bank account into which her scholarship money would be paid, and did it all with smooth efficiency so that the others looked on in awe at this young woman who seemed so at home already in a world far beyond their experience.

As they watched her, May seemed to be with them watching herself, equally amazed at her own cool achievements. She seemed to have grown a second self and this one had, for the time being, taken control. But in bed at night and at odd moments during the day, May came to and trembled at what was happening to her and her lack of control over it all and did not know if she could trust this other person to get things right. Practically, she knew it would work out perfectly, but this other May had pushed her aside and would not pay attention to her general nervousness and fleeting fits of pure panic.

In the end, she decided that she had better let everything happen according to plan. Once there, she would know if it had been for the best or was a hopeless mistake but she could not decide on the basis of a single visit to London.

The interview had been straightforward. She had set off on the train wearing the beret and gloves, but when she had arrived and found her way through the terrifying melee of the city to the college gate, she had felt a sudden moment of certainty that a beret and gloves would give a false impression and pulled them off and stuffed them in her bag.

The college was warm and smelled like school, and the corridors and the wood panelling reminded her of school too, so that she felt quite at ease. She was made to wait only five minutes in an outer room before being called in. No one else waited with her.

She was called in to sit in front of an elderly professor, a younger man and a woman who introduced herself as the Tutor to Female Students and who reminded May so much of her headmistress that the sense of being somewhere familiar was strengthened.

The questions were partly about work, books and

38

reading, with a few about her family and her background which she was aware were being asked for her own benefit.

'We want you to be sure you have made the right choice,' the woman said. 'And that you'll find your feet and fit in easily.'

'I'm sure I will.' May heard her own clear and confident voice and recognised it as belonging to the one who had brought her this far.

At the end of the interview she had walked down the long corridors and out into the college courtyard knowing that she had made a good impression and would almost certainly be offered a place and that her headmistress had known nothing at all in recommending the hat and gloves.

She had some time before her train. It was dark. Fog came off the river and wrapped itself fuzzily round the street lamps on the Strand. She stood and watched the buses and taxis and cars and people stream past her and smelled the smells of fog and petrol and knew that she had been right and that this was where she should be. She was excited, not nervous, she was looking forward, not worried about leaving her present life behind.

Years later, she remembered the moment in every detail, saw herself standing there in the middle of

London, felt the same feeling in the pit of her stomach. It only needed a breath of foggy air or the sound of traffic through busy evening streets to bring it back.

5

SHE LEFT the night and the stars and the empty spaces and crept back into the house and the terrible silence.

She stood in the kitchen doorway and for a second saw the dogs that used to lie by the range in coldest winter and the cat on the old crocheted wool cushion. The people round the table. John Prime in his shirtsleeves and braces, cutting cheese. Frank staring, staring. Berenice in something pretty. May herself was not there, she had already left and come back, an invisible ghost to spy on them.

Nothing had changed in the kitchen except that there was no one there, dogs and cat long dead and never replaced, John Prime dead, Berenice in her own home. Frank. But she turned her mind from Frank now.

And Bertha.

She climbed the stairs, holding the banister not for support but for comfort. How many hands had slipped over the rail, smoothing and smoothing but never wearing it out?

It was different. Even in this short time the body had slipped further down into death. It seemed to have changed colour, the skin to have yellowed and become more opaque. She remembered hearing about how everything flees the body at the moment of death, not only living cells but bacteria and microbes, how the air flees the lungs as oxygen evaporates, how decay begins, taking over what is left.

She could see it.

The body on the bed did not belong there now, did not belong in this place at all, and she could no longer relate to it. She reached out to touch one of the hands but drew back. She had nothing to do with this strange thing.

She switched off the lamp and closed the door, leaving it to itself and to the ongoing work that death must do.

In the kitchen she poured a beaker of water. The wind had got up a little more and was rattling the larder window. She took the water to the table and sat down.

She knew what she was doing. Everything had changed the moment her mother had died, but now it had settled and she clung on to what there was because once the calls had been made the next change would be greater and she did not feel ready for it.

She was fifty and felt older, felt a thousand years old and weary, and how would her life be now? She sensed that there would be things she might have to fight for and she had done all the fighting years ago.

There would be no fighting with Colin. He was too like their father, needing peace and ready to pay for it. Berenice would fight in her own clever, soft-footed way, the blade always concealed.

But Frank? What would he do?

Surely Frank would not come. He had too much to lose in a fight which must be all three of them combined against him.

Frank would not come.

The telephone was in the hall. It was put there when they first had a telephone thirty years ago, put where people used to put their telephones but where no one kept them now, out among the coats and in a draught. She had thought for a long time that one day she would have it moved, into the kitchen or the front room, but making changes to the way the house was and had always been had not been easy, even when her mother had finally taken to her bed.

But now, May thought . . . now.

The only change had been when the old heavy black receiver had to be changed for a push-button model, and in a moment of self-will, May had chosen cream because a cream telephone seemed stylish. But all a cream telephone did was become grubby.

It was grubby now.

'Hello?'

It was Eve who answered, dark-haired, brown-faced Eve who had been born old, like a hobgoblin in a story and then had had to grow into her ancient looks. Eve had become a nurse, abandoned nursing, married a farmer, abandoned him, moved away, come back and married the other stockman who worked alongside her father, and who was twenty years older. They lived in the next door cottage which was small and dark like Eve, and where they were as happy as children.

'It's Amma.' Amma for Aunt May. Even now the children were not allowed to call her May.

'What's the matter?'

It must have sounded in her voice. 'Is Colin there?'

'I'll get him. What's the matter?'

'Let me talk to Colin.'

Eve made an impatient sound with her tongue against her teeth.

'May?'

'She's gone.'

She heard the long sigh first, then he asked if the doctor was there.

'No. I don't have to get him tonight, do I? I don't think so. I'll wait till morning.'

'Whatever you think. You know best, May.'

I don't, she thought. I have never known best, I have always made the wrong decision, been asked and not known the answer.

'Do you want me to come now?'

He should have said, 'I'll come,' not asked her to choose. She could not expect him to drive thirty miles when there was nothing he could do because it was done. Everything.

'Have you told Berenice?'

'I rang you first.'

'Are you all right?'

'Yes.'

'You shouldn't be there on your own with . . . with her. Shouldn't you get the doctor now, then the undertaker would . . . shouldn't you do that?'

'I don't think so. There's no urgency. She's dead,

Colin. She can surely stay here the one night in her bed.'

Though as she spoke, as she said 'she' in her mind, it was 'it'. The body. Not their mother. Not Bertha.

'I could come after milking.'

'You do that, Colin, that would be best.'

'I doubt if Janet can get away.'

'No, no, she needn't trouble. Just you.'

'Right. Was it, you know, peaceful?'

'Oh yes. Yes, very peaceful. She just drifted off to sleep. It was fine.'

'Good. That's good. So I'll see you tomorrow, May.'

'Yes.'

'It'll be mid-morning. Sometime mid-morning.'

'Yes.'

'And you'll ring . . . Berenice.'

'Yes. I'll do that now. She'll come of course, but it will depend when she can get away.'

'I suppose so. Yes.'

'Goodnight, Colin.'

'You sure you're all right?'

'I'm quite sure. Goodnight then.'

Everything that could be said had been said. May knew that if she had needed him to come he would have driven over at once, but they understood one another well enough, she and Colin, she had spoken the truth in reassuring him and he knew it. She pictured him going to tell Janet, with small brown Eve listening, eyes bright with inquisitiveness, and Sara reading hunched in a corner of the sofa, not listening, not interested. Sara reminded May of herself in her youth, detached from everything going on around her. She had tried to talk to her sometimes, to show that they were on the same side, but Sara had recoiled into her privacy, looking at May with scorn.

The house was so still. Even the wind had died down now as often happened here. A wind would blow for ten minutes or half an hour then drop, leaving the Beacon quite silent. At other times it would roar up the hill and settle to hurl round the chimneys and crash the gates for three or four days or more, driving them all mad.

It was some time since she had eaten anything but she only wanted to drink cold water and when she did so strange thoughts came to her, that Bertha would never eat or drink again, that Bertha would never speak or sigh or smile again. That finally it was all over. Though she shied away at the last thought, fearing what might be to come, unhappy that the future she had longed for was now the present and she would not be able to live in it. It had happened before.

6

MEMORY IS random. The time she spent at the university was a series of moments which were illuminated in exact detail set between stretches of total darkness, and the moments were not necessarily important or significant ones. They had been caught in the passing beam, that was all.

In the final few days before she left the Beacon, John Prime had become almost entirely silent with her, not out of disapproval, she understood that, but from embarrassment that he had nothing to say about her future life, because he knew nothing. She might have been going to the moon. Bertha did not speak to her either but the reason for that was easy to explain. Bertha was envious and Bertha certainly disapproved. Bertha saw May escaping to somewhere of bright promise peopled by those who would turn her daughter's head and seduce her away from her family, causing her to look down on them and dissociate herself from everything to do with them and their life at the Beacon. She remained silent except when she let out short hissing remarks that darted in and out of her mouth like a snake's tongue. If you missed them they were not repeated.

From feeling sad that she was leaving and uncertain whether or not she was right to be doing so, May longed to go and ticked off the days in thick black ink on a little notepad beside her bed, leaving it out so that Bertha would see it.

She went alone. Her trunk had gone on ahead by British Road Service and she had only a small linen bag embroidered with purple irises by some forgotten aunt. John Prime drove her to the station in the pickup and as they turned out of the gate, May looked back to see if her mother was watching and waving her out of sight. But she was not.

Her father gave her a ten-shilling note and was glad when she said he should not wait for the train, he had too much to see to.

She knew of one other girl from her grammar school who was going to London, though Sybil Parsons had been in the parallel form and never a friend. But when May got onto the train she saw Sybil in a corner of the first compartment she came to and slid the door back at once, relieved not to be travelling alone after all, though she had not known until this moment that she had minded.

Sybil Parsons was knitting, the work growing out of a neat cotton bag. She was dressed neatly, in a plaid skirt and white blouse with a high collar. Her coat and a small grey hat were on the rack above her head and it was from the rack, an hour later, that she produced her lunch, a tidy parcel of greaseproof paper tied with string containing egg sandwiches, a neatly cut square of Battenberg cake and two small perfectly round apples.

May had rejected Bertha's offer of a packed lunch, saying that she would eat on the train, but when the attendant came down the car calling first service for the restaurant, her nerve failed her entirely and so she sat opposite Sybil Parsons, watching her eat the neat, crustless sandwiches, biting them with small snaps of her front teeth.

She had a flask of orange squash and when she had drunk some, offered it to May, after first wiping round the rim of the cup with a paper napkin.

May could taste the weak squash now, feel the cream Bakelite cup against her lips and even the lurch of the train as she drank.

*

London. She had been confused and unhappy from the first day, not by the city itself which she liked to walk in by herself, through crowded streets and empty squares, up side alleys and wide open green spaces. For that first term she spent most of her spare time when she was not in classes walking alone, and as it was dark early most of her memories of that time were of lighted shop windows and lighted buses, the smell of smoke and fog on cold air and the faces of strangers looming at her suddenly in the streets.

No, it was not London.

She did not enjoy living with other people in the honeycomb of college hall, where she made no friends because she could not learn the language of late-night gossiping and early romance. She shared a room with a pleasant, quiet girl called Frances Lea who was studying biology and left for the labs early and came home late after meetings of Societies – the Folk Dance Society, the Alpine Society, the Methodist Union, the Choral Society. May worked dutifully and attended lectures and walked through London. After some hesitation she joined the Film Society and sat in dark cinemas watching strange art films with subtitles that seemed to her as meaningless as rituals from a lost past. At a meeting she suggested they try Ealing Comedies or films starring Fred Astaire but was received with such coolness that she abandoned the Film Society and went to small cinemas alone to enjoy *Top Hat* and *Spring in Park Lane*.

She made the best of her own company but when the spring came she joined the tennis club and played in Lincoln's Inn Fields.

It was around this time that the terrors began. The first had come when she was waiting at a crossing in the Strand, and before the lights changed from red to green she saw the whole stream of traffic as a thunderous army menacing her and the people walking past as hostile enemies with staring eyes which bored through her body and into her soul. The lights changed from red to green perhaps twenty times before she was able to shake herself free of the terror enough to cross the road and then she ran for the safety of the college walls and a dark corner where she stood with her hand on the wall, and the wall seemed to be about to crack and crumble.

The terror left her as suddenly as it had come, so she decided she must be sickening for an illness and even went to the college nurse who took her temperature, pronounced her well and told her to have a quiet weekend.

In the middle of the night the terror woke her. It had not been a nightmare – she had come out of a safe and dreamless sleep into the knowledge that large ants were crawling over her body and eating the skin away. She put on the lamp, disturbing Frances Lea, who turned over two or three times, muttering.

There was nothing on her skin, but she inspected her arms and legs closely for any sign of bites or marks. When she lay down again she saw strange shapes behind her eyes, trees with branches that curled upwards and inwards and turned to ash and blood-covered beaches dotted with mounds of sand-covered snakes which stirred and coiled and uncoiled. Her own heart was beating extremely slowly and as it beat she felt it enlarging, swelling and filling out like a balloon inside her chest and stomach and finally growing up into her brain.

She sat up and felt calmer and in the end remained sitting up for the whole of that night, and by morning, felt tired but calmer and entirely herself.

The terror did not return for four days. Then, as she walked into the large lecture room, she saw that the seats were filling up not with other students but with white translucent shapes like boils which pulsated and began to exude thin trails of greenish pus. The pus ran down between the rows in a thin virulent stream widening as it moved and flowing towards her. She turned and ran down the corridor, down the great flight of stone stairs into the college entrance hall, but she knew that the stream was flowing behind her and gathering strength like a tide. She ran outside and through the gates and, dodging the people on the pavement, into a side street which led to the river. It was only when she was there, leaning on the Embankment wall looking at a huge barge going slowly past on the water, that she felt safe, for somehow the other tide had dried up and shrivelled back on meeting the great flowing Thames.

A few nights later she woke to find herself in the corridor with Frances shaking her by the arm. 'You scared me – you keep doing this, May, you keep on scaring me.'

'Doing what?'

But Frances shook her head, pushed her back into bed, then turned over.

The next afternoon when she got in from lectures she was asked to the warden's office.

She was referred to a doctor who prescribed sleeping tablets, even though she had no trouble sleeping, only with terror, and she could not find words to speak about it. The tablets made her thick-headed in the mornings and she found it hard to focus on the Reformation and Frederick the Great and Mussolini's policy, but the terror continued to strike her without warning.

Frances asked to change rooms.

May was put into a small cubicle on the top floor with a window so high that it allowed her no view except of a grey dishcloth square of sky.

She cried much of the time she was there and then the terror followed her down the escalator of the Underground station and onto the train. It took the form of extremely thin men without faces who walked sideways and could slide themselves into her body like cards into a pack and talk to her in obscene language. She got out at the next stop and ran, but of course it made no difference, by then they were in place.

It was a beautiful spring, mild and sunny, and May walked through the parks and sat on benches and took her work to cafés where pigeons flocked onto her table for biscuit crumbs, but the pigeons had running sores and red gimlet eyes which saw into her soul and she was forced to cross to the other side of the city, miles and miles of walking to get away from them.

Once a fortnight Bertha Prime wrote her a letter, on one side of the paper, asking questions rather than giving news of the Beacon, and as May could not answer truthfully she did not reply at all.

When the first-year examinations came she was very confident, because although she had failed as a human being living in London she had worked hard, the only short-lived trouble being the effect of the sleeping tablets, which she had thrown down the lavatory when she dreamed of being eaten from the head downwards by Frederick the Great at a state banquet. But when she sat down in the exam hall and the first paper was delivered to her desk, she saw that it was written in a menacing and unfamiliar language which contained threats and abuse. She folded it forty times into a tiny pellet, picked up her things and left. When someone called her name she ignored her.

She left London the next day and, sitting in the corner of the compartment, wished that Sybil Parsons was opposite to her with neatly wrapped sandwiches. But Sybil Parsons was happy at her own college in Regent's Park and would not be home until the very last possible day. She had sent May one postcard suggesting that they might meet if she, Sybil, ever had 'a spare half-second', but May had not replied to that either and had sensed Sybil's sigh of relief from the building on the other side of the lake.

7

THE ODD flares of memory from that year
remained.

Once, she had sat down on the bottom step of a
large house on her way back to college after a late-
night walk, overcome with terror and feeling safer
huddled against the railing there, and a taxi had
slowed and stopped. A woman and a man had got out
and while the man had paid the woman had come
towards the house. She had stared down at May.

'What are you doing there?'

But then the man had come up. 'Poor girl, poor
girl, whatever is wrong with you?'

He had been concerned until the woman had said,
'No, don't talk to her, don't touch her, send her away,
send her away.'

But before he could do as he was bid, May had

spared him, sensing that he would have to obey the woman, his wife presumably, and be ashamed to do so, and had got up and run away down the road. Glancing back, she had seen his face in the light of the street lamp, looking after her, troubled.

One day she had walked down an alleyway off Fleet Street and, seeing a door ajar, opened it further and found herself looking into one of the newspaper printing works with the machines rolling and the place an inferno of noise. She had felt the machines were about to lift steel claws and draw her down into them and had turned away and run without looking where she ran so that she was almost killed by a bus. The bus was a red dinosaur lit up inside and roaring.

Once, she had seen the Professor of Medieval History stop and pee against the wall at a side entrance to the college and she had been unable to move but had to watch as he buttoned his trousers and adjusted his coat before turning away. He had not seen her. He had not known that he was known, she had thought afterwards.

But there were very few lighted pictures between the long dark stretches of that single year.

8

A ND so she came home and it was as if that year
had never been. The worst she had to endure was
the expression on her mother's face, of satisfaction
and smugness, for Bertha had been right all along and
May was not fit to be away. John Prime said nothing
but one morning after she had been back a few days he
had brought her a mug of tea early and said he was
going up to look at the sheep on the top, which meant
the fields farthest away from the Beacon, and perhaps
she would like to go with him. She had drunk the hot
sweet tea quickly and slipped out of the house
carrying her shoes in case her mother should hear and
stop her, and they had travelled together on a golden
morning when the sun was already hot as it rose and
the larks spiralled up out of sight, singing, singing.

The terrors had not come home with her and she

slept as deeply and dreamlessly as she had as a child. It was only the days that seemed a dream, for she glided through them and it seemed to her that as she did so she was like a wraith and left no mark. She was neither happy nor unhappy, she was suspended, apart from all feeling. She spent most time with her father out on the farm, riding with him, watching him, occasionally helping with this or that small thing, and his unquestioning and accepting company soothed her. Otherwise she helped in the house, doing what her mother asked, not thinking, making no plans. The summer drew on and the days passed by, the swallows soared over the roof of the Beacon and the house martins nested under the eaves. The barn owls reared young and flew, cream-faced and on silent wings, past her window at night.

It was at night that May walked out by herself. She waited until the house was still and left through the back door, sliding the bolt carefully and then crossing the yard to the gate and so into the fields or down the lane. It was a dry summer and the nights were sweet and cloudless, the stars brilliant. When she was out like this, her detachment became an intense sense not so much of happiness as of rightness and satisfaction that she was here, in this place. She went a long way, up onto the high hill among the sheep, whose pale eerie faces appeared out of the darkness close enough for her to feel the warmth of their breath on the night air. She felt ageless and suspended in time and wished for nothing, hoped for nothing, simply was, quietly there.

No one ever found out about her night walks, or so she thought, and the broken sleep seemed never to leave a trace upon her.

The one person she talked to about what she might do with her future was Berenice, who was so much younger but still nearer to her in age than anyone else in the house except for Frank, with whom she could talk about nothing simply because Frank talked to no one. Frank listened and watched and otherwise scarcely impinged on life at the Beacon.

She and Berenice spent hours upstairs in May's old room which Berenice had taken over the day she had left for the college, Berenice brushing her hair or leaning out of the window, May sitting on the bed putting forward this or that plan.

But no plan was satisfactory. She did not want to go back to studying, even if there had been a college near enough for her to travel to every day; she knew that her mind would have turned to sawdust with the boredom of the jobs available in the town, in shops or offices; she did not have the temperament for nursing; she could not teach without finishing her course.

'You'll have to get married,' Berenice had said at last. 'There are plenty of men to marry.'

To May, marriage meant exchanging one house for another, possibly one farm for another, one lot of chores for another, and then the possibility of having children. She did not think she liked children enough to make them the focus of her own life for the next twenty years and could not picture herself feeling enough for any man to do the same.

'You should have a boyfriend by now.'

Berenice had a boyfriend, Alan Meersey whose mother had died when he was born and whose father looked after him alone in a flat over the fish shop he ran. Alan Meersey was the fourth of what was to be a line of boyfriends stretching far into the future before one ever became a husband, but May knew that it was Berenice who had the knack of acquiring boyfriends, because she liked them. She liked boys more than girls, she said, it was quite simple.

But nothing fitted May. Besides, while she was at the Beacon the terrors stayed away. Sometimes she could barely remember them or understand the power they had had over her. Here she felt safe. She was aware that in lingering at home, perhaps waiting for something to happen, something that would solve the problem of her future for her, she was betraying herself and everything she had once wanted and might have had. She dared not defy the terrors which she knew perfectly well would overcome her if ever she made a second attempt at independence.

Once she almost told Berenice about the terrors but held back partly because she did not have the words to describe them, partly because she was ashamed of them, but mainly because instinctively she knew that Berenice was too young and also that she was happy and May had a duty to protect her from the shadows.

Now, May sat for a long time at the table in the kitchen feeling the absolute silence of the house and her aloneness in it like a cloth wrapping around her and shrinking back into it for safety.

But in the end, she returned to the telephone in the cold hall.

'Berenice?' she said.

9

WHEN BERENICE was eighteen she had simply said that she was leaving home and had gone two days later, to the town ten miles away.

Bertha Prime had wept. May had gone to London to study, something which Bertha could understand and of which she was secretly proud, though she would never have said so. But Berenice had left home to live with the family of someone she had been at school with, but nevertheless barely knew, in order to work in a florist's shop, and so Bertha's resentment was bitter and, she felt, entirely justified. When Bertha was a young girl she had been pretty with a small, heart-shaped face and a slender neck, but as she grew into late middle age the flesh thickened and dropped and formed pillows beneath her jaw. She looked at Berenice who resembled her more closely than any of the others and saw her own young self and her resentment blazed up into anger. If Berenice chose to leave her home and family without good reason then Berenice would have to beg to be welcomed back. But Berenice did not beg. She loved her work, became the manager of the florist's shop and had a succession of boyfriends of her own age before meeting Joe Jory when she was twenty and he was forty-nine. Joe Jory played the flute in a folk band and was the only man in the whole of the north to read people's futures for money. He wore a thin ponytail and a thick beard and a strange hat with a band embroidered in bright runic lettering. He and Berenice married and went to live five miles from the town in the opposite direction from the Beacon, in one of the old quarrymen's cottages. They were as happy as children and so did not bother to have any of their own.

A few times they had made the journey to the Beacon in Joe Jory's dilapidated van, but Bertha had been unwelcoming and put her resentment forward like a hook on which they could not help but catch themselves, so they did not bother to come again but just sent cards at Christmas and on birthdays, at least until John Prime's funeral.

It was Joe Jory who had told Berenice about Frank. He was the first to find out.

*

'Berenice?'

'She's gone then?'

May closed her eyes.

'Are you on your own?'

'Yes. Except . . .'

'That doesn't count. Not any more. Do you hear me, May? Listen – you're on your own. She doesn't count any more. It won't sink in yet but when it does you'll know what it means. You'll be free then.'

'I . . .'

'You'll understand later. You've rung Colin.'

Berenice just knew. Always knew.

'How long ago?'

How long ago was it? May shook her head, as if she could shake the sense of time back to rights, time which had run away and lost itself since it had happened.

'Not long,' she said at last. 'It just – happened. I was outside. I wasn't with her.'

'Doesn't matter. Not your fault.'

Wasn't it? The enormity of having let Bertha die alone after having promised so many times made her go giddy.

'Listen, you don't have to fetch the doctor or the undertaker tonight but I would if I were you. You'll lie awake thinking about it. Get them to come, May.'

How was it that Berenice could manage everything,

sort it out at once, when she was the youngest and had been shielded from life by the rest of them for years?

'You can talk to Colin about the arrangements.'

'Yes.'

'Funeral.'

'Yes.'

'It would be about a week to ten days, depending.'

Depending?

'How busy they are, mutt.'

Berenice even knew what she was going to say when it was still unformed by her mouth.

'Oh. Yes.'

'Is the bottle of brandy in the front room cupboard?'

'I suppose so. Yes. I don't know.'

'Have a drink. Not more than one but have one. A good measure. Yes?'

'Yes.'

'Then phone the doctor. He has to come first to certify but you can ring the undertaker to come straight after. Take her away. Do it before it gets really late.'

'Yes.'

'May? You'll be all right now. You will.'

'Yes.'

'You know what else I'm going to say.'

'Yes.'

'You're not to think of telling him. Not to ring him or send him a letter, nothing. He has no right to know. He forfeited that.'

'Yes.'

'But we should put it in the *Advertiser*.'

'Oh yes. I'll do that tomorrow. Colin will help me with that.'

'Good. You'll be all right, May.'

'Yes.'

She would be.

She put the receiver back and went into the front room. The fire had not been lit in this grate for, what, two years? There was the cold of death in the walls. The brandy was there, in the cupboard. She took it into the kitchen. Poured a good measure. Drank half of it. Then she went back to the telephone.

Berenice had said what she had thought, that Frank shouldn't be told. They would surely all agree on it. Colin would and that was everyone. She, Colin, Berenice. Frank had forfeited this and every other right.

The doctor came within the hour, the old Dr Price not his son, which was a relief to May because he had been the one Bertha had known, the one who had come out to her for years of her odd fits and panics as well as in the last few years to see her when he could do nothing but pretend.

'Now what about you, May?' he said, following her up the stairs.

'I'm all right, doctor, I'm fine.'

'You said you weren't with her?'

They stopped just outside the bedroom door.

'I'd only slipped out for a few moments. She'd been fine all afternoon – all day – I'd never have gone but she'd been fine.'

'No one's blaming you, May. No one ever could. You've been a load-bearer for many years. Besides, you know they have a way of waiting to die till they're left alone. Why that is nobody knows, but it's a fact. Maybe to spare the living, maybe for some other reason.'

'Is that what she was doing? Waiting to die until I was out of the room?'

'It could be so, May, it could be so.'

They had been speaking in low voices which seemed odd for they could not waken Bertha now. Respect, May supposed. More respect. Why were the dead to be more respected than the living? She did not think she had ever received respect from a soul throughout her life, but perhaps she would not have known it anyway.

The body had changed again. It was smaller. The

flesh was shrinking further back from the bones and the whole frame seemed smaller and slighter in the bed, as if life had been a weight and space-filling like air in a balloon and now that it had gone what had contained it fell in upon itself.

She looked at the doctor. Looked away. She was growing used to the density of the silence in the room now.

It took little time.

'Your mother might have wanted to rest awhile here at home, May. Are the others coming?'

'Not tonight. I don't know how long they might be. It would be best if she went, wouldn't it?'

She saw that he understood.

'Then telephone for the undertaker.'

She could not tell him that she had already done so.

At the front door he said, 'Take another small nip of the brandy, May, and then no more.'

As he went away she saw the lights of the undertaker's van coming towards her up the hill.

10

THE DAY Frank Prime had left the Beacon at the age of nineteen he had changed. The silent, watching boy had begun to talk, while still a watcher; the one who had slipped like a shadow in and out of rooms became the man who laughed loudly, spoke loudly and became the centre of attention with great ease.

Like May, he had gone to London. Unlike May, he felt that he had come home from the moment he stepped off the train.

He had left school at fifteen and gone to the technical college in the town for two years to study surveying and after that become apprenticed to the local council buildings department, but on arriving in London the Frank Prime who had done all of this was shed like the

71

skin of a snake. He had saved enough money, carefully and quietly, to rent a couple of rooms and take his soundings of London, walking about the city as, if he had known it, his sister May had done and the walking had eventually led him, too, to Fleet Street but not to the hell pits of printing machines. Frank Prime had walked into three newspaper offices in search of work and in the third had found it. He became a noisy, sociable dogsbody in the newsroom.

From the first day he had found himself, as he had found his city, and he seemed to explode with cleverness and confidence and a passion for news and for words on paper, a passion which he had never known for the figures and measurements, lengths and breadths of surveying.

He got in early and left late but joined the rest of them in one or other pub from the beginning, and in the pubs he listened and stored away gossip, stories, confidences.

Over the next few years, Frank ascended from office boy up the ladder to reporter and then, after moving papers, to senior reporter. He specialised in crime, and in addition to travelling round the country to the scenes of major crimes he spent days in the Old Bailey at trials. His face became familiar. He had regular bylines. He seemed to love and be immersed in his work.

And then he married, a widow called Elsa Mordner who had money and a large and gloomy mansion flat at the South Kensington end of Earls Court. Elsa had a sallow skin and a sour expression. She was tall, with long bony Gothic hands and feet and, until she met Frank, had been increasingly lonely and without anyone or anything in particular on which to spend her money and her attention. In Frank, it seemed that she had a docile, cheerful, companionable man who was out of the flat for the major part of the day as well as for those nights when he was away reporting. Somehow, her long days spent shopping or reading or going to galleries and tea shops, which had been mainly ways of filling the time, were transformed simply because she had someone who would be coming home to her. After a year of marriage, the two or three close friends she had noticed that her complexion was less sallow, her expression less sour, and concluded with relief that this marriage, contrary to all their expectations, was completely suitable for her.

Frank had never taken her to meet his family and indeed almost never spoke about them, whereas she told him a great deal about her own in Munich and took him to visit them twice. The visits were not a success because the family could not understand why Elsa had married an Englishman not once but twice and sensed, rightly, that whereas they were from generations of solid burgher stock Frank Prime was not. Such things mattered. He was aware of the polite, correct and entirely chilly atmosphere and regressed to his old childhood self, silent and watchful. Elsa did not care for the person her husband turned into when they set foot in her home country and thereafter she went to see her family alone.

In Munich, Elsa's parents lived, as they had always lived, in a large, high-ceilinged apartment in an old building, so it was natural for her to have bought the same in London, but the apartment was the one thing about his marriage which Frank hated. He hated living on one level. Going to bed on the same floor as that in which the cooking was done and in which he ate and read and watched television felt wrong, and although he was entirely happy in London he missed having outside space of his own, in summer most of all. Even a small garden would have done.

Intermittently over the years he raised the subject with Elsa, who was quite uncomprehending.

'I lived in the country,' he would say. 'I lived on a farm. I lived among open spaces.'

So with Elsa's money they bought a small flat by the sea. Meanwhile, in London, instead of pacing up and down a garden path somewhere, Frank paced up and down the long rooms of her mansion flat where the lamps had to be lit almost all day and the bedroom often smelled of roast lamb or frying eggs.

Frank communicated rarely with his family at the Beacon. He did not so much think as brood about them. Elsa no longer asked anything but never ceased to find it strange that anyone should not wish to keep in touch with parents and siblings, not speak to them on the telephone, not write or visit, not want to have news. She was not a possessive woman and would have been happy to share Frank with whichever members of his family he chose as she had wanted him to be part of hers. Indeed, what followed might never have happened if she had not read out loud at breakfast a couple of lines from one of the weekly Munich letters. She usually did this and Frank usually listened in silence and without comment.

They had been married for fourteen years. Frank was now head of the news desk and no longer went out to the courts or away reporting crime. He was too senior. He ran the most important part of one of the most important national newspapers. He wrote leaders from time to time. It had taken a while for Elsa to understand that leaders, written anonymously, were more prestigious than news pieces with a byline.

'Listen,' Elsa said, 'my brother is writing a book!'

She went on, translating as she read the letter from

her mother who still lived, alone now, in the same old apartment.

' "Peter came to see me as usual on Tuesday and made me very pleased and proud. He has been asked to write a book about some aspect of the law, which I do not fully understand, I confess, for a publisher in Bonn who I know is very highly regarded. So, we will have an author in print in the family!" '

Frank looked at his wife. Her long face was proud. It was then that it came to him, the whole thing at once so that he was taken aback and had to leave the room and walk round the flat. 'So, we will have an author in print in the family.' Well, so they would have two. The book was there in his head, whole, as if someone had planted it, a shrub in the earth. He had no idea where it had come from or why, but he took it and he would make use of it. It excited him.

He got off the bus halfway as usual and walked the rest of the way to Fleet Street and noticed nothing around him and, when he got into his office, he stood looking out of the window high up, looking down on the street and knowing, knowing, hugging his secret to himself. It had changed him.

He went to a stationer's at lunchtime and bought two large writing pads, ruled, feint with margin, and a new pen. He had always used a typewriter and now a word processor, but he knew instinctively that he would be writing this by hand.

He would take time off work and write in their flat by the sea in Suffolk. They were due there the following weekend and he would begin then, while Elsa went shopping and visited friends in the town, took part in coffee mornings and bridge afternoons. Her social life there was far richer than in London. Frank never joined in such things, nor was it expected.

He walked the first half of the way home more quickly than usual.

Three days later they drove to the coast. They arrived just after two and fell into their routine, Frank going out to buy fresh fish for their evening meal and to walk back along the shingle beach, Elsa remaining in the flat to make up the bed and air the rooms. It was a bright early-spring day with a bitterly cold east wind off the sea, the tide rushing in.

He got back to find Elsa lying in the doorway of the bedroom, a pillowcase in her hand. She was dead, he knew it the moment he touched her, her face twisted a little to one side, eyes open and startled.

Within six weeks, Frank had resigned from his job, sold the London flat and moved what he needed to Suffolk. He had no need to work now, whether or not the book was successful. But he did not doubt that successful was what it would be and in this he was fully justified.

It took him a much shorter time to write than he had expected. Once he began, the pen took on a life of its own and he watched it race across the paper, telling, inventing, creating detail after detail. Every evening when he read over what had been done that day he was astonished at how convincing it was, how the stark descriptions and bleak conversations conveyed truth. At first he wondered where deep inside him it was coming from, this story he did not know he had to tell, but then he simply accepted it and continued.

It came together with its title, like a child born already named, but he had to choose how to send it out into the world. Deciding took little time.

On the day he finished, he went for a walk along the road that ran beside the shingle beach. It was grey and cold and the waves were white-flecked. He was surprisingly content being alone and scarcely missed Elsa, but he was aware that both men and women living alone can become misanthropic and reclusive and he would need to give thought to his future. Perhaps he would marry again. If he did so, it would be on different terms. He was now wealthy and he was inclined to believe that the book might also make him famous. He had the stronger hand now.

He wondered if he would write anything else, if there were other things stored away in the dark cupboard. He felt no urge to investigate. If they were there, they would come to the surface.

From his time in Fleet Street he knew a couple of publishers and one literary agent and, wanting an opinion and someone else to handle the business side of things, he spent the next ten days typing his manuscript and making some small changes and corrections. Then, he packed it, posted it to the agent, and very deliberately put it from his mind.

11

I<small>T WAS</small> Joe Jory who found out about it first. After he had driven Berenice to work every morning in the old van he often had time on his hands. The band had more gigs in the winter and the telling of futures was a dwindling business, but Joe Jory was resourceful and liked ferreting about, so he began to make bits of money here and there from buying and selling. He bought from here and sold to there, went to auctions and flea markets and had a special line in following up the death notices in the local paper. If he read of a person who had died at an advanced age, he tracked down their address and went there, offering to clear. Nine times out of ten there was remaining family or else the house was empty or he got sent smartly away, but then there were the occasional times when he struck lucky. Berenice privately admired his enterprise while chastising him to his face for profiteering from the dead when they were barely cold. Joe Jory took it all in and carried on, knowing that with Berenice words came cheap.

On this morning he bought a couple of papers and then went into Dusty Dolly's where he sometimes had breakfast and read his way carefully through the small ads. Dusty Dolly's was full and smelled of damp coats and frying bacon.

There were a couple of death notices which he ringed in biro, and a few ads for jumble sales, which only rarely yielded him anything worth buying. After he had done the work, he had a second mug of tea and began to look through the rest of the local paper.

He did not recognise the photographs at first but that was not surprising as he had not known any of the family at that age. The first was just the author as a small boy; the second, the author with the rest of his family sitting in a field somewhere round a picnic cloth, a tractor and trailer in the background and hay stooks. Joe Jory looked more closely.

John. Bertha. Colin. Frank. May. Berenice.

When he left the cafe he walked, through the town, up the hill behind it, down on the other side, back along the road past the mill, down into the town again. An hour of walking did not help to clear his mind, did not help to order his swirling thoughts, did not help him to decide what he should do. He did not know if he should go to the shop now and tell Berenice or wait until she got home that evening, or whether he should tell her at all. No, he must tell her before someone else did, someone outside the family, or someone made an unpleasant remark, dropped a hint, head to one side, pitying. Perhaps May would telephone her, or Colin; they would tell her and spare him. Perhaps she already knew?

No, he was certain that she did not. There was no way she could have kept this to herself. She did not know.

He sat on a low wall outside the post office, took the paper out and read the page again.

The Cupboard Under the Stairs.

Berenice could not have kept all this to herself either, so it could not be true. Perhaps a little of it was true?

He refolded the paper. He went back to the cafe. Another mug of tea and he would fetch Berenice out of the shop, take her home and tell her there, break it to her in his own words first then show her the paper.

The cafe was full now and he had to sit at a table with a couple of women. One of them glanced at him. Glanced away.

It wasn't the girl, Tina, who brought his tea over, it

was Vic the owner. Vic didn't serve tables but he was serving now, bending down to him as he set the mug on the table.

'On the house, this,' he said.

Shame surged up like bile into Joe Jory's mouth. This was the start then, the first thing Frank Prime had done to them. People knew. People would talk and blame, or talk and pity, talk and wonder, talk and stare. Talk.

He sat in front of the tea, not drinking, turning over what he should do. He did not want Berenice to see the paper before he had prepared her. Had Colin seen it or May? Bertha, he knew, was not likely to do so and it could be kept from her without too much trouble. He thought of telephoning Colin, but what if Colin had not seen it, did not take the paper and so he was the first to – to what? Break the news. Better he did it than a stranger.

In the end, he decided that it was not up to him to tell anyone but Berenice. She could talk to the others, let them decide what to do between them. If there was anything at all that could be done.

He walked slowly along to the florist's shop. Outside on the grey pavement the buckets of bright flowers had been freshly watered. The sun had come out and caught the drops of it here and there and made tiny rainbows. Joe Jory stood looking at them.

He should call Berenice out and show them to her, so that she could enjoy them before what he had to say changed everything.

But she saw him through the window. She was wrapping some long-stemmed roses in white tissue. He watched her. She was concentrating but she glanced at him a couple of times, bright-faced, smiling. So no one else had been in before him. She did not know yet.

He waited, looking at the drops of water on the bright flowers until the customer had left and the shop was empty and then he went inside.

12

AFTER BERENICE left home, May found a job, though only in the village, working at the convent which was hidden out of sight at the bottom of the wooded valley.

Water came flowing down the steep and stony track through the trees and fell without ceasing into a stream which flowed on, widening to a river as it ran past the convent and away between steep banks. May answered an advertisement in the window of the village shop. She cycled along the path that skirted the wood and wound down, more gently than the rushing water, towards the convent buildings. She had never been here before. She pushed her cycle the last yards and then stood, looking at the bowl of sky and the water falling and the flat stretch of gravel path leading to the front door. It had a strange atmosphere, desolate in spite of the sound of the water.

But when she had been asked inside she found not a desolate place at all, though one which was quiet and calm. The nuns smiled at her. She saw them doing ordinary things, cooking and writing and sewing and sweeping the floor. Somehow, she had not expected that, just silent women saying silent prayers.

She was to help in the kitchen and the garden and with the chickens, because there were too few of what they called Lay Sisters at that time – some were too old, too sick, two had recently died. She had expected someone to ask her if she was baptised and confirmed, if she prayed and went regularly to church. No one did. She had expected nuns to be stern and stony-faced but several smiled.

She went home feeling pleased.

Bertha Prime had pinched in the corners of her mouth and said that May wouldn't last long and that it was not natural for a lot of women to live cooped up together.

For seven months, May cycled the six miles to the convent and back every day and when she was there she was perfectly content. She did not mind manual work, she liked being outside better than in and she found the nuns kind and friendly. She grew used to the bells and the way they stopped whatever they were doing every so often to kneel and pray or go to the chapel. When that happened she carried on with her own work and no one suggested that she should do otherwise. She did not have much conversation unless about a job just done or needing to be started, but she had time to think; otherwise the routine was gentle and soothing and the time slipped by as smoothly as the water in the stream.

At the end of seven months, just as the cold of winter was beginning to ease, Bertha Prime slipped in the yard and broke her leg, and a week later, had a slight stroke.

May left the convent. She would be welcome back whenever she could go, they said, when she could be spared from home. But she never would be. May knew that.

The convent in its deep bowl beneath the woods and beside the water became a place she returned to sometimes in her mind and she often dreamed about it. It was a solace to her. But she never returned. Just come to see us, they said. She did not.

After that she knew she would never take any job away from home, that she would be here to run the house and look after her mother forever, or what passed as forever. She had had her chance of freedom but freedom had not been for her, she had been afraid

of it, and life under the rule of fear was not life worth
having. At the Beacon she was safe and not unhappy.
As her mother turned in on herself and never fully
recovered from the first stroke, so May took over the
reins of the house, made the decisions, looked after
the everyday work, saw to paying the men, and once
a week took the bus into town to shop. Later, she
bought a car, against Bertha's wishes, and learned to
drive rather quickly, to her own surprise, and then
she was able to go to the supermarket further away
and to visit Colin and Janet and, once she was
married to Joe Jory, Berenice. She enrolled for a
night class in local history, knowing that she should
not waste her brain, and borrowed books and joined
the Local History Society. Twice, she presented
papers to their meetings, one of which was printed in
the biannual *Local History Journal*. So long as May
kept things running smoothly at home and she
herself was looked after and not left alone at night,
Bertha accepted all of it without resentment, though
without comment or interest either. May was quite
alone in her activities outside the Beacon and inside
it, alone in her own mind. But if it was a lonely life
she grew used to that, and it was not a sad one. May
was perfectly well aware that one or two men had
found her interesting and even attractive and that if
she had chosen to do so she could probably have

married, but she did not choose. She liked her home and, if she ever thought about it, she felt it would be pointless to exchange one house and its upkeep for another, strange one and to alienate and upset her mother. Colin said nothing but Janet had sometimes asked her obliquely if she was quite 'all right' and did she not ever think of leaving the Beacon should the opportunity arise, and Berenice was more open and told her she should find a husband before it was all too late. 'You should, May, it's what you need. It's only normal. You should do it.'

But May knew that she would not. She was an intelligent woman. She knew what others said of her, and her family, but she ignored that knowledge and kept on with her life. She was not ungrateful. It might be pedestrian but she had a home, food and comfort and a share in the farm, though money never came easily. They had not moved with the times at the Beacon. One day in the January of a bitter winter, she was standing at the window looking out onto the yard and saw two of the cowmen and her father dragging a zinc feed bin containing a sick sheep across the frozen snow with ropes, towards the barn. Their ancient coats were tied at the waist with binder twine and their caps, soaked with the snow, were blackened and shapeless. She felt guilt and shame that their lives were so hard, that they had not enough help, not enough decent machinery, but had to drag animals in bins across the snow.

Knowing how the kitchens at other farms were, May worked to make sure that the one at the Beacon was clean and as tidy as it could be, with the range always lit and the table well scrubbed and cleared of milk bottles and old sacking, half-eaten bread loaves and rusty nails and cans of sheep dip. She grew plants on the window ledges and washed the covers and curtains and scrubbed the tiles on her hands and knees. Left to Bertha Prime the place would have fallen apart. Sometimes, John Prime would help her with the kitchen jobs, drying the pots and filling the range, but he came in every evening exhausted and fit only for eating and then nodding off for an hour in the chair before going to bed. He was a man who said little, though he smiled at those he knew, and once, he told May that she was 'the best in the world'. She wished she had known that he was going to say it because she would have prepared herself to listen carefully, but instead the words were spoken and over before she had realised and the memory of them grew faint quite quickly. 'The best in the world.' She gazed at him occasionally when he was asleep in the kitchen. He looked older than his years, as all the men who worked on the land did, and his hair had thinned early. His hands were calloused and reddened, the nails broken down. Manual work outdoors was hard on the body. The cold burned through to the men's bones and they sweated in the sun. She felt sorry for him, though he knew nothing else and never expressed a desire for it either. But her mother angered her, resting much of the day and giving up all of her work to May, though she was surely capable of doing more than she pretended. She still mended a few things and knitted, but mainly she sat looking out of the window and doing puzzles in the daily paper, eating what was set in front of her and saying little to anyone. Once May had begun to drive she had suggested outings to the village, to the town, or to see Colin or Berenice, but Bertha would go nowhere and after a time May did not ask. She was relieved. She liked driving her car, liked being alone and free of everyone.

If she had been asked she would have said that, yes, she knew it would have to happen, of course she knew, as who could not, but naturally the blow fell when it was furthest from her mind.

It was one of the first warm days of April when the green shoots of wheat were spiking through and the yard had dried out after the months of mud. She had hung out a line of washing. The kettle was on ready for when the men came in for breakfast. She was putting out some scraps of bacon rind and crumbs from the board and, as she did so, noticing the touch of sun on her face. The tractor pulling the trailer was turning into the gate and she watched it, her father glancing round to check the distance from the post, though he knew it by feel, could have turned in blind and never made a mistake. The trailer was loaded with bales of wire because they were repairing the fences after winter.

May watched as the machine stopped and then shuddered as her father switched off the engine. He waved to her and began to climb down, but instead of jumping to the ground from the metal step, as usual, he hesitated for a second and then fell.

She hesitated, thinking he had twisted his ankle on the step or missed his footing, thinking those things at the same time as knowing that he had not, that the way he had fallen and the way he lay was because of something else.

She knew that he was dead before she knelt down to him, but by then two of the other men had come into the yard and May stood up and started shouting.

It was all pointless, everything that happened then was quite pointless, but it had to be gone through, the telephoning, the doctor, the ambulance and covering him with an old coat and rubbing his hands and talking to him. He was dead. He had been dead as he fell, they said, and May had known it.

But she had stayed there with him until the end, watched him go, out of the gate and turning into the lane for the last time, the awkward turn which he had made on bringing the tractor in. The last time. She had talked to the men and to the doctor and still lingered outside, putting off the moment when she had to go in and tell her mother, the moment when everything would change and the future she had always dreaded would begin.

13

S HE DID as she had been told and drank the small second glass of brandy and then no more, sitting at the kitchen table in the house full of silence and remembering that last time and how she had felt the tightening of the threads that bound her here.

Tonight, she felt the freeing of them. Bertha was gone. May knew that it would take her a long time to grow used to her absence and to the empty time she would have to fill. After her father's death they had gone on for a while as before, the men doing the same work, the tractors turning in and out of the yard, the animals in the stalls and sties, chickens still pecking about the grass behind the house. Then, one by one, things had been let go. The cattle first, then the pigs. It was three years before the sheep were sold off after a particularly hard winter. The chickens remained a while longer, and the geese had only gone the previous spring. One of the men had left the day of John Prime's funeral, two others had lasted only a year more.

That funeral had been the hardest day of May's life. She had not realised how much she needed her father's presence to make life at the Beacon bearable until she had watched the coffin being lowered into the ground. She had loved him and looked to him for comfort and strength and the occasional word of praise. Gratitude did not need to be spoken, she knew he was grateful to her.

The short drive back to the house with Colin and Janet had been made in silence, but then the place was full, John Prime had been well respected and everyone expected a wake, people coming from some distance. For an hour or so the Beacon had been full of warmth and large bodies and strong voices, glasses raised and plates emptied of food.

There had never been a party at the Beacon before, and to her shame she had even enjoyed it and been proud for her father. Colin had worn a stiff suit and looked uncomfortable. Joe Jory, who owned no suit, had draped his cap with black ribbon and made a bow of black ribbon into some manner of a tie. And Bertha had sat in state in the front room and received everyone, gracious as a queen, dabbing her eyes with a folded handkerchief. But what May never knew was that Bertha's grief, though formally expressed, was sharp and bitter. She had been married to a man she had loved and respected and now her future, like May's, was stretched bleakly before her.

Perhaps if she and May had spoken about him, if they had spoken about anything more than trivial things, they would have found out at least this about one another, that there had been such love.

Life changed. Life stayed the same. Bertha Prime retreated back into herself. The animals went. The men left. May spent more and more time alone. The house seemed emptier than it had ever done before and few people called. May went to see Colin and Berenice because they preferred it that way round and Frank remained in London.

Yet May was not unhappy. She liked life to be even and uneventful, she needed the routine of days and to know that it would be winter and spring, that it would be dark early and late and then light in the mornings with the long-drawn-out summer evenings. She looked for the return of the swallows and house martins and swifts to their nests and the frogs crossing the yard on their way to the pond and waited for the berries to ripen and the nuts and leaves to fall, feeling each small repeated change as her security.

Even Bertha's demands were regular and formed the backbone of May's routine. She had to take her early-morning tea and get her up, wash her, help her to dress and to her chair and later to make lunch and settle her for her afternoon rest. Make tea. Settle her for the night.

Nothing disturbed the tenor of their days or the quiet in which they passed them.

14

WHEN JOE Jory told his wife that she should telephone the girl who came in part-time to help in the florist's and tell her that she was needed today, at once, Berenice did as he said out of astonishment because such a thing had never happened before. He had nothing to do with the shop. He never came to it. The girl had arrived within twenty minutes, and Berenice and Joe Jory had left in silence, walked to the van and driven home, and until they were inside he had told her nothing, other than to reassure her that there had been neither an accident nor a death.

All the way home he had wondered how he could protect her, even while he knew he could not spare her. He could only nurse her as the blows fell. Colin would find out, if he had not already done so, but Colin was strong and he had Janet.

And then there was May.

The rain had stopped and a weak sun was shining onto the back of the house. Joe Jory opened the door and set a chair there. Then he handed the newspaper to Berenice and went quietly away, to potter about in his den within earshot, not able to bear to watch her face as she read.

It took her a long time to read it, mainly because she had to keep going back to the beginning, and to the headline and to the photographs, trying to take in what exactly had happened, what Frank had said. But in the end, when she had read it all the way through slowly twice, she let the paper fall onto her lap.

Sensing a change in the quality of the silence, Joe Jory came out of his den, pulled another chair beside hers and took hold of her hand. She turned to look at him. Her face had changed. She had aged, somehow, in those fifteen minutes, had lost the bloom of innocence which had always been such a delight to him. Her eyes were wary.

'But it isn't true,' she said, 'none of this is true. All this. All this Frank has written in his book . . . if he has written these things.'

'Oh, he's written them all right. He has written them.'

She looked down at the paper. '*The Cupboard Under the Stairs*,' she read. 'He's written a book about us called that?'

'Yes.'

' "The Story of One Boy's Brutal Childhood." '

'Yes.'

'But . . .' She looked down again. At Frank's photograph and at the picture of the cover of the book he had written, and at the two photographs of them all, and of the Beacon. They took up a whole page of the paper.

'But . . . it isn't true. What Frank says about us . . . about . . . our home. These terrible things he says about himself. None of these things are true.'

'No.'

She shook her head. 'How can this be happening? How can my brother have written these things? How can he have done this?'

Joe Jory stroked the back of her hand. There was nothing at all that he could say to help her or to change any of it.

'Why has he done this? Yes, that's it, isn't it? It's *why*?'

'Yes.'

She sat with the sun on her face, feeling her husband's thumb rubbing the back of her hand, the newspaper on her knee, and she could not make sense of any of it. But at last she said, 'A newspaper isn't enough to go by, do you understand me? I have to read the book, don't I? I have to read Frank's whole book.'

Three days later, Joe Jory brought it back home with him, having driven over ninety miles to the nearest city with a bookshop. He had kept it in its paper in the old string bag he used for shopping and looked neither at it nor inside it all the way back. It was not for him to do that, it was for Berenice.

It was late afternoon when he walked into the house and by then she had spoken twice to Colin and once to Janet. But they were certain that as yet May did not know anything at all.

The book Frank Prime had written told the story of his unhappy, lonely and abused childhood at a farm called the Beacon and of the misery almost day and night of his life there until he fled the place. It blamed his misery not only on his parents, John and Bertha Prime, but on his siblings too, either because they were party to the infliction of Frank's suffering, or because they shared in his torments and did nothing.

Everyone was named and there were so many details of dates and times and places and of what he had to endure that it must, surely, be truth rather than fiction, for who would make up such stories?

There is a cupboard beneath the stairs at the Beacon and I cannot now go into any house which has a similar cupboard or think of that particular one without pain and a return of the memories and the nightmares. I have given my book its title because that cupboard symbolises everything that was bad about my boyhood, sums up every tiny cruelty, stands for every fear.

It is a large cupboard because the Beacon is a large farmhouse and it has a few bits and pieces at the back – as I dare say every cupboard under the stairs does – the leg of a broken chair, a stock of brandy, an ancient leather suitcase, some bits of wrapping paper. It has a sloping ceiling of course, and the ceiling comes right down to the small angular space at the very back into which I used to crawl and where I sat for so many hours, pressed against the plaster and smelling the dirt and dust. I do not remember when I was first pushed into the cupboard but I cannot have been more than a toddler, a little boy of barely two, and I know that it was not part of some childish game. It was my father, John Prime, that huge man with the raw red hands, who put me in there, for some babyish misbehaviour, and dropped the latch. If I cried about anything or made some little complaint, I was put into the dark there. Why? Why me? None of the others was ever pushed into that cupboard. Colin was not a bad boy, as bad boys go, but he was up to far more mischief about the place than me and he was told off, but only lightly, only in a jokey tone. He was never punished as I was punished.

I can never forgive my parents for what they did to me. I am a man who is terrified of the dark so that I can barely go out on winter evenings and I have slept with a lamp on beside my bed for years. Imagine what that did for my marriage – though my wife, Elsa, was very understanding. I never told Elsa the half of it.

I cannot forgive my father or my mother, Bertha, for colluding with him – for she never protested, never tried to protect her little boy.

But what about my brother and sisters? Surely they would have tried to stop it happening and to let me out of that dark and dreadful hole? No. Instead, they pushed me back inside it and even shut me in there when my parents were not around, threatening me with dreadful horrors if I managed to escape of my own accord. But it was the things May told me, things about what lived and breathed inside the cupboard under the stairs, that were the worst of it, monstrous, evil, lurid, hideous creatures and spirits. These creatures insinuated themselves into my mind and burrowed their way down into my subconscious and fed on my imagination. I can conjure them up now. I can smell and feel and hear them and I am still afraid, though I know they do not exist and were only the awful fantasies invented by May.

The cupboard under the stairs is not the worst of it, not by a long way, but let it stand for everything they did to me through those years of my growing up. John and Bertha, Colin and Berenice and May took away the innocence and the happiness, the peace of mind and the whole childhood of their own brother Frank and, now that Frank is a grown man, he cannot forgive them.

I dedicate this book to every boy who was ever made to suffer in the cupboard under the stairs.

In his own cottage, sitting alone, Colin Prime read on. The rest of the family were in bed but he could not have slept until he had finished his brother's book, though it was years since he had read anything but the newspaper, from time to time, and the stock reports. He had no head for reading and no leisure, but this was different, this book held him in his chair for an hour, two hours, scarcely able to breathe in the quiet kitchen.

At first what he read had puzzled him because he had taken it to be a story, in spite of their names being true, and he had not understood why Frank had not thought to invent names for his characters. But as he read on it became clear, though only in one sense. Clear that Frank meant them to be themselves and their parents too, and the Beacon and the farm and the village and the village school to be true to life, yet not clear because the rest was an invention. What had Frank meant? To tell a story or remember the truth or to muddle the two?

But as he read on, Colin saw that there was no confusion, not in Frank's mind, not in his intention. He told the story as if it were true. He told their lives as children in every detail so that anyone reading it who knew them would recognise them as themselves, and anyone going to the Beacon would know every room and the items in those rooms. But what he was telling as if it were the full truth was not the truth. It was not the truth as Colin knew it or as it had ever been. It was not Frank's truth because none of the things he described had ever happened. Not the beatings nor the taunting, not the hunger nor the thirst nor the punishments, not the way his father had made him run round the farmyard naked in the gale and rain when he was five years old, not the tale of his being locked in the shed with the bull or made to eat the swill from the pig bucket. It was not true that Colin had locked him in the cupboard under the stairs time after time or that they had all taken him up to the attic and whipped him raw. It was not true that his mother had goaded them on and spat in Frank's face and that he had had to sit under the kitchen table while the rest of them ate and had only been given the scraps they dropped down to him. It was not true that he had been made to walk four miles back home from school because John Prime had thrown him off the tractor. Not true that May had jammed his fingers in the door and gone on closing it. That he had never had any new clothes of his own but only Colin's cast-offs after they were worn out, and shoes that were the wrong size and made his feet bleed. Not true that May taunted him because he could not spell Berenice. Not true that. Not true. Not true. Page after page after page. Not true.

But Colin had to read on to the end, every lie, every page that was not true. He could not stop until it was after three and he had to get up again at five thirty. Then, at last, he closed the book and laid it down on the arm of the chair and put out the lamp and dozed in front of the dying fire until the dawn came up because he was too tired and angry, too hurt and bewildered, to go upstairs to bed.

15

No one knew how to tell May, left at home with Bertha, managing everything.

'It's May,' Colin said several times a day to Janet, when he had found words to talk to her about it.

Janet too read the book at a sitting, but Janet was shrewd and understood Frank better than any of them. 'He was always fly. He used to look and hang about and not speak to you. It doesn't surprise me. It shocks me, of course it does, it's a terrible thing to have done, but it doesn't surprise me. Not in Frank. Frank might have done anything, I've always thought that.' She was not claiming special knowledge, or being wise after the event. Janet spoke the truth. She had always believed Frank capable of something but of course she could never have imagined this. Nobody could have done so.

'It's May.'

'She has to be told, Colin. Why try to protect her? She's a grown woman, and clever, she went to university, she spent a year away from home. You seem to forget that about May. You have to show it to her.'

But Colin had shaken his head.

Berenice had driven over to their cottage, leaving Joe Jory, who was getting ready to play at a folk festival and in any case felt that he had done all he could and it was no more of his business except in so far as it might affect Berenice.

They sat round the table, Colin, Janet, Berenice, and the book was there in front of them. The cover, with its sepia photograph of a small boy in shorts, his hair cut raggedly and too short, his head bent, beside the shadow of a low door, seemed to make a fourth, a spectre at the table.

'What's he done it for?' Colin said. 'That's what I can't get my head round. Why? What's it for?'

'To cause pain.'

'Why would he want to do that?'

'His sort do.'

'What sort? I don't know what you're talking about here. This is my brother, my only brother, and he writes a book about his childhood – our childhood, mine, my childhood – and it's all a pack of lies. I don't know why, that's all there is to it.'

'Does it matter why? He's done it and everyone knows about it, thanks to the paper.'

'You can't blame them, it's a good story.'

'Everyone will know.'

'There's nothing to know.'

'What will they say?' Janet asked.

'No smoke without fire.'

'Precisely.'

'But there is.' Colin got up and wandered about the room, a huge man, making every piece of furniture seem too small. 'That's exactly what there is. Smoke and no fire. There never was a fire. Was there?' He sat down again.

'Not to my knowledge,' Berenice said.

'Isn't that – well, I suppose, the point?'

They both looked at Janet.

'You say it wasn't to your knowledge. But maybe things happened to Frank you didn't know about. Well, that could be it, couldn't it? You can't just dismiss it.'

'I can,' Berenice said.

'The thing is, he accuses us. We shoved him into that cupboard, we made him run round our yard with no clothes on and whipped his legs, we threw him off the tractor. Us three. This is what he's saying so I don't see that he can have suffered in secret, not at all.' Colin got up again, walked about. Sat.

'I just want to get this quite straight,' Janet said. 'Nothing happened to either of you of this sort? You weren't beaten – well, not more than any of us were – nobody shut you in this cupboard, you weren't laughed at and sneered and jeered at and singled out for unkindness?'

'No, we were not. Nothing like that, ever. They were good parents to us. To all of us.'

'Right. So it's made up.'

'Of course it's made up.'

'We just come back to why. Why has he done it?' Colin said, and ground his thumb into the tabletop.

'Money. People get paid for books. And fame.'

'Funny sort of fame.'

'Look, I don't care about him, Col, I don't give a toss about Frank and why, I care about us. I mind what he's done to us with this. I mind what he's done to Dad's memory and to Mother, what it's going to do to us with the people we've always known. We've lived here all our lives, we know everyone, we've never had anything to be ashamed of or anything to hide.'

'Still haven't.'

'But it'll seem as if we have. Some people will believe it, people always do, and they'll look at us and point and gossip behind our backs.'

'Sticks and stones.'

'No, Colin, no, words *can* hurt you. Frank's words have started hurting us already and it'll just get worse.'

They fell silent and each of them stared down at the book and the book seemed to grow bigger and bigger as they looked at it, to become a vast, bloated, hideous thing, and then to come alive and smirk and mock at them.

The book that Frank had written seemed larger and more powerful than anything in the room, anything in their lives now and in their lives as they had been, because it had changed them and the change could never be undone. The book had power. They understood that. The book had made what was innocent seem sinful, had tainted them and the past and had destroyed the innocence in which they had all lived until now.

And so they sat on, surrounding the small and terrible thing which was Frank Prime's book.

But of course May knew. She might be alone with her mother at the Beacon but she was not a recluse. The local paper was delivered every week, though principally for Bertha's interest rather than May's own. May was in the habit of skimming it first, over her milky coffee and before taking it upstairs to Bertha, and so found the page about Frank's book, together with the photographs.

She was mortified and she was angry, but from the first sentences as she read them she was not altogether surprised. Frank had always been the watcher, the one who listened behind half-open doors, the one who played small, mean tricks and then smiled. Quiet, waiting Frank.

Nor did May wonder why he had done this, since it was quite clear to her that, although he liked money, he would like fame and to be talked about even more, and it would not trouble him that the talking was not full of admiration.

She had to keep the paper from Bertha, and she was anxious about Colin and Berenice, feeling them to be more vulnerable than she was herself and both almost wholly innocent of the malice and devices of a man like Frank.

May cared nothing for what anyone in the village or further afield might either think or say because surely anyone who knew them at all would know that what was written could not possibly be true. They would take it for the fairy story it was, for fairy stories had wicked parents and unhappy children locked in dark cupboards or else sent out alone with a crust of bread into a snowy forest. Frank had written a fairy story, but because he was what he was, had thought it more amusing to use his own family and their home and their true names.

*

When Berenice telephoned, May was ready and perfectly calm.

'Of course I mind,' she said, 'of course I'm angry. But there is nothing to be done about it but hold up our heads. It will pass. Everything does.'

'Shouldn't it be stopped? Surely it can be stopped if it's all untrue?'

'How? The book is written and published. How can we stop it? Who would take any notice?'

'But it isn't *true*.'

'A lot of stories aren't true.'

'But he's saying that it is. He isn't telling a story.'

'We know that he is. Everyone else will too.'

'How can you be sure?'

'I just am.'

Berenice sighed. She wished she had let Colin do this, as he had half offered. Perhaps he would have been able to make May understand.

'You haven't let Mother see the paper?'

'Of course not.'

'People were talking about it in the street – in the cafe.'

'People will. Oh, Berenice, let it run its course. *We* know the truth.'

'*Do* we?'

'What?'

113

'I just . . . wonder. Maybe some of those things did happen.'

'None of them did. How can you honestly think that? You and I know we didn't do any of them, Colin is the kindest man on earth – and could anything like that have been going on without our knowing?'

'No.'

'Of course not.'

'I'm so angry, May.'

'So am I. We have every right to be angry.'

'But what are we going to do?'

'Nothing. We can and should do nothing. Let Frank wonder. Let him stew and wonder what we're thinking and what people are saying and what might happen. Let him. That will be his punishment.'

'I don't think it's enough,' Berenice said.

And thinking about it all the rest of that day and in her bed at night, nor did May.

None of them had been prepared for what happened. They had expected people to stare but not to stare with such knowing and judgemental eyes, so that all three of them were forced to look away at once, or down to the ground, burning with shame. They had expected some people to come up and tell them that, no, they did not believe any of it, that they had known John Prime for the good man he had been and Bertha for the difficult but still good mother, known Colin, known May, known Berenice. Knew. But few did, though a couple of people came into the florist's shop and bought something small which Berenice knew was entirely out of kindness or at least pity, and one of the men who worked with Colin made some gruff remark that he understood as sympathetic. But on the whole, people stared and summed up for themselves and kept their distance.

May retreated even more into herself and the routine of life at the Beacon, looking after Bertha and shopping some distance away where she was not known and might not meet anyone who would stare. She read the book. It shocked her more than she had expected or could have explained to the others. She was disgusted by the things Frank had invented and the lubricious way in which every detail was told. If it had all been true and written by someone quite other, she would have been shocked because she did not see why such things should be bruited abroad. They were terrible and if they were true should remain private, and the victim should work out his salvation with some trusted adviser or well-trained professional.

Colin and Berenice had been angry and hurt at once but it took more time for May's feelings to harden. She felt little for herself, the bitterness was mainly on behalf of their dead father and their mother who lived in a lonely, twilight invalid world, mostly of her own devising.

She thought about Frank for a long time, walking about the farm and up onto the hill where she was unlikely to meet anyone and where she sat on one of the low stone walls from where she could see the roof of the house, thought and delved into her memory of their childhood. But she came up with nothing, nothing at all but contentedness and a certain amount of hardship, though no worse than that suffered by many round here and by no means as bad as some. Had one of them been mocked and teased, it would have been May herself because she had been clever, but her cleverness had simply been accepted, as had Berenice's prettiness and Colin's strength and loyalty. That was how it was. That was how they had been.

When she returned from one of these walks May went to look at the door of the cupboard under the stairs. Frank had described it well enough, and when she looked inside found that he was right about that too, though it was even smaller than he had implied and no child could have been pushed very far to the back. The latch was loose too and the door easily opened.

But the cupboard under the stairs was only a symbol. She wondered if one small thing had happened to Frank, which had then seeded itself like a weed, gradually taking over his mind.

No. He had done this with malice, to hurt them, but John Prime was beyond hurt and in a different way so was Bertha, and as for the three of them – they would neither be hurt nor fooled. And they could answer back, May thought suddenly. They could do that.

16

THEY EXPECTED it to be a nine-day wonder and that they had only to hold their heads high until it all died down but in this they were wrong. Things not only went on but they grew worse because as the book was published Frank gave interviews in newspapers, on radio and television, and spoke about them without any reticence, repeating the lies and basking in the sympathy of those who talked to him. New photographs of him appeared alongside those of the small boy and of the whole family. The book became a best-seller and then, in paperback, a bigger seller and there were posters advertising it, bearing the photographs, on hoardings and at railway stations.

A year and a half passed during which none of them grew accustomed to it or learned to ignore the expressions on the faces of those who had once been friends and were still neighbours. They had only one another to speak to now, but that was one thing they could still do. They spoke on the phone, usually May and Berenice but sometimes Colin, too, or Janet on Colin's behalf, and told one another of this or that which had happened because of the book. Without these conversations and the times when they gathered either at the Beacon or at Colin's farmhouse, they would have suffered even more. But it was a hard time and the hardness of it showed on their faces.

The year after the story first appeared, a film of Frank's book was announced and the papers were thick with it all over again, with the names of directors and producers and actors.

'Actors pretending to be us,' Berenice said, 'and John and Bertha. Actors pretending they know us. And where will they film them? They can't think of coming to the Beacon?'

Perhaps they had thought of it, but no more than that, and it was said the filming would take place in Ireland, or Scotland, or on the Isle of Man or even in Spain – though it was Ireland in the end.

Perhaps I will die before it happens, May often thought, so that I won't have to endure this any longer.

But she did not die. None of them died but went

on, holding their heads up and talking together and making the best of it, which was all they could do.

Bertha grew more feeble during this time and spent most and then all of the day in bed, lying plucking at a piece of knitting she had asked May to start for her, or twitching at the corners of the magazine she still had delivered though never read. She slept and looked at the sky beyond the window and her mind wandered to places May did not recognise when she described them. She became quieter and less demanding but she hated to be left alone and May found it difficult to get out for long to shop, and impossible, soon, to be able to go and see Colin and Berenice. They had to come to the Beacon, but that was not easy for them and so the times they all met together to talk and for comfort were fewer.

Their lives became narrower and each one of them looked inward and felt inclined to solitude. Janet noticed the change in her husband, Joe Jory in Berenice, but there was no one to notice the change in May.

Frank's life changed too.

For a time, Frank Prime was interesting to a great many people. He was known, people demanded his company, his opinions were sought after – at least on the subject about which it was felt he had written so movingly and with such truth. Every now and again, at some lunch or on a television programme, when people surrounded him and listened to what he said, Frank felt a small discomfort, as if a shoe were pinching slightly, and he recognised it as guilt. But it would always pass and he felt no shame. For he came to believe in what he had written. Those childhood memories which had been ordinary and frightening were overlaid by the childhood of the boy he had invented. He felt a sadness on behalf of the small child he had created.

Money came in from the book and more money from the film of *The Cupboard Under the Stairs*, more money than he had expected. But he spent little. Sometimes the shoe pinched and he thought that he should give some of it to Colin and May and Berenice, none of whom had ever had much to spare, but the pinch eased and he did nothing.

He waited for the sky to burst open and for fire to rain on his head. Every morning he woke expecting angry letters in the post or even a ring at his doorbell and to find one of them waiting. But he heard nothing at all. The longer the silence went on, the more he thought about them and wondered how they had reacted and what effect it had had upon them, and the silence and the fact that he could not know frustrated him and became a constant irritation like an itch beneath the skin. It exercised him more and more until he thought of little else. He woke wondering about them and as he went about his day they were with him, but silent and out of reach.

Colin, he thought, would bear it without complaint and little comprehension. He might be puzzled enough to think back to their childhood and go over certain days, delve into certain memories, but on the whole Frank thought that Colin would react little, would simply go on with the business of his life.

Berenice had always been a pert-faced, sugar-coated, manipulative little thing, and it would be Berenice who would scream and shout and try to chivvy the others into anger and violent reaction. Berenice would weep and storm and be full of self-righteousness. She would not stop to think but if she did she would, of course, believe nothing because her own childhood had been so rose-strewn, its paths so smooth and easy. Nothing had ever happened to Berenice. Others saw to that. It had occurred to him once that Berenice might even enjoy the notoriety; he clung to that and soon it was firmly fixed in his mind. Berenice was proud. She was written about, someone had played her in a film. She had probably read the book several times and marked certain passages and gone to see the film more than once too.

The only one he feared was May. He could not guess at May's reaction. May had ploughed her own furrow. May had had her chance, had gone away and might have stayed away as he had done, but she had been fearful and weak and scurried home. He had no sympathy for May. But if there were ever to be any retribution he knew that it would come from her.

Over time he justified his book by allowing all the inevitable tiny slights and knocks of childhood to grow and harden in his mind as he went over them, elaborated them and added detail. He allowed his feelings to overflow as he remembered, until he could no longer have identified what was true and what he had invented. The others could have set him right but he could not talk to the others and so he came completely to trust himself and his own ordering of things.

He was detached from all the new people who seemed to have gathered round him, and from what they said. And then the letters began to arrive and it was hard, at least at first, for Frank to be detached, for people wrote telling him their most intimate and terrifying secrets, the stories of the abuse they had suffered at the hands of parents and friends, sisters and brothers, neighbours, nannies . . . the list went on, everyone in the world, it seemed, had been beaten and starved and kept in the cold, every little boy had a cupboard under the stairs and every girl a locked cellar. The writers addressed Frank with relief and gratitude. To them, he was the only person who might understand, the first one they had been able to tell. They wrote page after page and they were unbearable to read. They called him a brave man and a saint. As the book grew in popularity and then when the film was shown, so the letters increased in number and length and in the horror of the stories they told, the secrets they spilled, the nightmares they recounted.

At first he read them all. At first, he replied, though saying little, only making a formal acknowledgement and giving a few words of thanks or understanding, but as more and more letters came, he skimmed them and before long ceased to read them at all but tore them up or burned them immediately, and certainly he no longer answered. But his silence seemed only to increase the number of letters. The writers seemed to be banging on his door and shouting at him to notice them, recognise them, speak to them, like the angry, unnoticed, neglected children they were. He felt as if he was drowning in the letters and the weight of their distress, bowed under so much pent-up unhappiness which he had somehow released.

Finally he asked his publishers not to forward any

more and then the letters were merely answered with a printed acknowledgement, but the flow barely paused.

He still lived in the flat he and Elsa had shared. His neighbours went on with their own lives in ignorance of who he was and what he had done, but when he stepped into the streets he was quite often recognised and stared at and sometimes followed. People went up to him in cafés and shops and began to talk to him, to thank him, to pour out their stories. He felt oppressed by them and went out less and less. He slept badly. He missed Elsa then, Elsa's straightforwardness, her complete lack of self-absorption, her brisk kindness. He had a lot of time in which to remember Elsa. He understood her now. He appreciated her.

But there was no Elsa.

In the end, he closed up the flat and went abroad, first to Europe but then, on a whim, to South Africa, where he settled in a house overlooking a bay and tried to write a second book and failed and after that sat in the sun and looked without much interest at the sea, and so the months passed and all the time he wondered about Colin and Berenice and May and how they had coped with what he had done to them, what they thought about him. He felt like someone shut out of a room in which everyone was discussing him but to which he would never be admitted and when he pressed his ear to the door all he heard was a dull and indecipherable murmur.

But they were not talking about Frank. If there were murmured conversations they did not mention him. Between Colin and Berenice and May now his name was never spoken, and they got through the days as best they might, working, eating, sleeping, waiting for sufficient time to pass in which the memory of it all would fade and even, by some, be quite forgotten.

And time did pass and some did forget. But Frank could not. Instead, as he sat in the sun and wandered about the beaches and drank in the bars, he remembered more clearly and in more vivid detail the things of his childhood, so that he seemed to be living at the Beacon again, to be walking about the rooms and touching the furniture, sleeping in his old bed and eating at the kitchen table, smelling the smell of the beasts in the yard and feeling the movement of the trailer beneath him as he rode up the hill behind the tractor with the others, the air fresh on his face. He could hear their voices. He could see the small mole on May's neck and Colin's finger where the nail had come off and the bright yellow of Berenice's ribbons. He heard their shouts as they came whipping

126

down on trays and boxes through the snow and his knee burned where he had skidded across the ice in short trousers.

Things he had not known he remembered were there, after all, and had only been hidden at the back of a drawer or put away in the attic and now they were all spread out before him so that he could not forget them again.

His nights were disturbed by the voices. People who had written letters visited him to read them out loud and the scenes they described were presented to him like plays that he was forced to watch. Small children cried and hid their faces behind their hands, but the tears came through their closed fingers and the voices began to call his name. They asked for help. They told Frank that he was their only friend and that he alone could save them. They begged and pleaded and wept and he could not get away from their anguished faces, and the voices, when he woke, sweating, were still speaking and crying softly in his ears.

He fled back to England. He had long since sold the flat by the sea, and now he hated the open spaces that had once spelled freedom. He moved into a London flat at the very top of a house with a skylight that let in light and brightness and a small balcony on which he could sit looking over the tops of the trees to the

Heath. He changed the old, heavy, dark furniture, spending a great deal of money on new, pale-painted cupboards and chairs with light covers, on white rugs and bright pictures. He had plenty of money. The flat was airy and quiet. But the voices and the faces could not be sold or otherwise disposed of and were there, released into the clear, clean spaces of their new home.

He never slept easily now. Small children pressed in on all sides in his dreams, the unhappy, piteous, damaged children of the letters. They implored him to help them, wept and held out their arms to him and then became angry and violent towards him and shouted out his name in hating voices, blaming him. He got up and walked about the flat and, sometimes, even dressed and walked the streets, hearing the sound of sirens, seeing the amber glow of the distant lights. Cars passed him and cats streaked in front of him across the road and he went on walking until he was exhausted, but when he returned to the flat he dared not lie down for fear of the dreams.

He thought of going back to South Africa, or else travelling to another country, to Chile or New Zealand or Japan, but he let the thought go, having the sense to know that the children would fill his dreams just as well there and that he had no escape from them.

*

The letters were all answered for him, but once or twice his publishers sent one on because it was a different kind of letter, perhaps from someone who knew him, which was how he received the announcement, clipped from the local newspaper, of his mother's death.

17

'She should come back here,' May said. 'It's still done. It's always done. For people to pay their respects. I don't understand why you think we should do anything else.'

Colin and Berenice were silent, not catching her eye.

'You think it will still make a difference? Of course it won't. It's over – what Frank did is all over and forgotten. People don't remember that now.'

Though she knew that they did, for how could such things be forgotten?

'They know that none of it was true.'

But they did not.

'They'll want to come as usual and we should have the coffin here. She should go from here.'

'Oh yes,' Colin said quickly, 'I agree with that. Of course she should go from here.'

'It's having the coffin here . . .' Berenice said. 'Perhaps it would be best if the undertaker brings her here and we just follow.'

'They came to see Father. You remember how many people came.'

'That was before.'

'Before Frank.'

'Mother was respected as much as he was. It would be wrong not to do what's always done.'

There was sudden quiet so that they could hear the faint whirring of the chimney cowl.

'You do what you think is best, May.' Colin got up. 'It's up to you.'

'We should agree. I don't understand why you're objecting.'

'Because,' Berenice said gently, 'it would be a humiliation if no one came.'

'I want her to be here. It isn't right without her.' Though May had felt the emptiness of the house and her own freedom since Bertha's death as a longed-for blessing.

'You decide,' Colin said, closing the door behind him.

They sat on in silence, the two sisters who were so rarely alone together, and the quietness of the house

131

settled on them and calmed them so that they felt in tune with one another and friendly.

She has changed, May thought, changed entirely from the pert-faced, pretty, spoilt little girl who demanded attention and praise and played off each of us in turn against the others. She has not grown up in any way I expected except that she is still pretty. I suppose it is all thanks to Joe Jory.

She has not changed, Berenice thought, time has brought her back to the sister she was when we were children, afraid of most things and under our mother's thumb. She had her chance and tried to take it and failed, and after that she retreated into the safety of this house, our parents, the past and her old self. Why? Was it the fault of anyone at all?

She looked across the table at May. She has a pinched, sour face, and perhaps nothing truly good has ever happened to her, nothing to transform and enrich her, none of the tremendous surprises of life.

And then it occurred to her that perhaps Frank had been right in one way, that what had been done to May *had* been a cruelty, though one she had always and fully accepted. They should have sent her back to London on the next train, thrown her into the sea and forced her to swim, as birds drive their young away.

They took her back because it was good for them, not good for May.

Was Frank right?

She shook her head. The sun shone on them and the grey hairs glinted like wire on May's head. But Berenice's hair was golden.

'What are we going to do?' Berenice asked.

May was silent.

'If you think she should come home, she should come home. Even if no one comes to pay their respects.'

'*We* will be here.'

'Shall I come to stay the night with you?'

May looked up in surprise. 'Why?'

'You might not want to be alone with the coffin.'

May laughed. 'I was alone with her alive for all those years,' she said. 'I was alone with her after she died. I can be alone with her again.'

'Then I'll come in the morning.' Berenice stood up.

She did not understand May. She had never known what went on behind the thin pinched face and the narrow spectacles and she never would. May did not change. May had always been a book which was closed and padlocked.

*

They brought Bertha's coffin home to the Beacon six days after her death and in the morning May had prepared the room, with fresh flowers brought over by Berenice and tall candles, though the day was brilliant and the sunshine put out the light of them.

The coffin was open in the old way. That was right, May said, and what she would have wanted, as it had been for Bertha's parents and for John Prime.

When the men had gone May hesitated, suddenly anxious about going into the front room to be alone with what she could not now think of as her mother but was something quite other, a dead body. On the night Bertha had died and when she had been lying in her own bed, she had been there with May, she herself, the woman, her mother. Now it was different. The body in the coffin was no longer Bertha.

But in the end May did go in and forced herself to look at the pale shrunken face and the slightly puffy eyelids, the tight jaw and the hair combed tightly back from the dome of the forehead. For a moment the sun was clouded and the candles stirred, their light flickering briefly across the waxen face, and May half expected her mother to open her eyes and stare into her own, the lips to move and speak, in order for her to say that something was wrong or make a demand.

The sun came out again. The room brightened. Bertha Prime lay dead.

May put on a cotton frock and her blue jacket and waited. Drinks were set out on the sideboard and she had made sandwiches and a cake; there were biscuits, sweet and savoury, cheese and fruit. She had opened the front door first thing and left it open for people to come in.

No one came until, at a few minutes to twelve, Dick Strong, the old cowman from John Prime's early days, drove in through the gate in his ancient Ford and wearing the black suit he had had since his own father's funeral sixty-seven years before. He was small and thin as a chicken and the suit was vast on him, hanging off his shoulders and falling in folds around his black shoes. He stood looking down into the coffin for a long time, then turned away and waited for May to offer him a drink, whisky, which he drank at once before going out into the farmyard and standing there, looking around at the empty barns and byres, his eyes watering, though whether from old age or the sun or even grief May could not have said.

She thought it possible that Dick Strong, who lived alone and saw no one, might be the only person in the county who knew nothing at all about Frank's book and would not have cared if he did.

No one else came until first Colin and Janet, then

Berenice with Joe Jory arrived less than half an hour before the undertaker, who closed the coffin.

The sun shone on the cars as they slipped out through the gate and made the awkward turn into the lane and on their faces through the glass and on the white and yellow flowers, bright on their mother's coffin.

18

HE DREAMED a dream of such vividness and clarity that for an hour after he woke from it he could not stop trembling, and it was then he made up his mind to travel to the funeral. He knew of nothing else that might save him. But it was a long way and he did not have a car any more; the journey was complicated and it was so long since he had been up there that he did not know the line to the town had been built over years before, so he had to get a taxi. He recognised the town well enough, though it had spread out; there were the usual blocks of houses where fields had been, but the little he saw of the centre was familiar. The town was built on a hill that sloped down to the river. It was prettier than he had remembered, but then, the sun was shining.

The taxi driver took a new road to the village and now, because there were only the hills and fields and small clumps of woodland, sheep and stone walls, he quickly lost sense of where he was and none of it was familiar. He might never have been here in his life before.

He had intended to go straight to the church but as they turned into the road leading to it, he saw that the cars were already outside, the back of the hearse open. The service would have begun and he could not walk in late by himself, interrupting it, having them all turn to stare at him. He told the driver to go back and take the road leading to the Beacon, but at the bottom of the lane, had him stop. He paid and watched the taxi until it was out of sight.

And now he remembered, the beauty of it and the loneliness of it together, and as he walked slowly towards the deserted farm he understood why he had hated it and why he had gone away and sworn never to come back.

It was the same. But not the same. He walked in through the gate and saw that there were clumps of grass growing between the stones and that some of the stones were sunken down and broken, and there was grass growing out of the roofs of the cowsheds and two or three doors had come off and were lying on the ground and others swung open, half off their hinges.

One trailer, its wheels rotting and overgrown with weed, was in the far corner by the tin barn, but there were no other vehicles.

It was silent. That was the strange thing that made him stand still in the middle of it all. Swifts still dived down into their nests in the roof slates of the farmhouse and swallows in and out of the sheds, but they were noiseless in their flight and there was not a stir of a breeze through the silent summer afternoon.

Frank looked about him slowly and after a while he found that his eyes were full of tears. He walked into the pigsty where there was still the faint sour smell of the animals and round to the stables where he saw wisps of hay from the iron manger rusting on the wall. The shadows were hard and dark across the broken cobbles of the barn floor. Above his head he saw a row of nests, perfect half-cups of clay moulded to the beams. In the corner by the old privy, where the nettles came waist-high to him, there was the sharp stench of fox. The only animals here now were wild and came and went freely, their lives untouched by humans.

He wondered if the door of the house had been left unlocked, as it always used to be, and whether he

139

should go in if so. He went towards it and the sun blazed about him.

The door was not locked. He touched the knob with his finger. Somehow, going inside would break the spell and would bring him face to face with everything and not least the truth.

He went from empty room to empty room and each room was sun-filled and he wondered as he walked quietly about why he had hated it so much that he had needed to hit back in whatever way he could, at the house and everyone he had lived with here. As far back as he could remember he had felt a misfit and as if he had been dropped into the wrong place, and the feeling had only strengthened as he had grown up. Of course he had told no one. What could he have said which would not have made them simply laugh at him? He had always believed that they laughed at him in any case.

He stood in the hall. The place smelled different. It smelled of emptiness. Did May live here alone now? He had no idea what any of their plans were because he knew nothing about them. He never had known.

He tried not to think about the book that had come out of him spontaneously, like some sort of effusion which he had not been able to suppress. It had controlled him, having a life and will of its own, and so he felt no guilt about it or responsibility for it. But how could he explain that to them?

He had come to his mother's funeral but too late, and there was nothing else for him here now. He should never have come. Had Bertha known about what he had written? Had anyone told her? Was there even a copy of his book in the house at all? He had not seen one. The only books had been the old ones in the glass case, untouched for years, and a couple of library books in May's bedroom.

There had been no reaction at all, no one had written, and he even wondered now if they might not know about the book. It was another world up here, people lived narrow, inward-focused lives.

But someone would have told them, someone in the town, some old acquaintance or relative, someone. They could not be ignorant of what he had said.

And then he heard the sound of cars turning into the yard and it was too late. He stood in the sunlit front room beside the table of food and drink covered in white cloths and waited for them to find him.

It was Colin who came in first, barely recognisable in his dark blue suit and tight collar, his body thicker than Frank remembered it, his hair thin on a head which looked wrong bare of its usual farmer's cap. Colin saw him at once and his face reddened from the neck up. He stopped dead, and at his shoulder, Janet and May, who came in together, stopped and for a few seconds there was absolute silence. In the hall behind them the voices of Berenice and Joe Jory died.

They heard the clock tick.

Then May looked round for help. But no one could help her.

'It had already begun. I was too late for the funeral so I came on here,' Frank said at last.

They remained silent.

No one else had come back, though Eve and Sara had been in the church.

Most of the food would be wasted though the drink would keep, May thought. Yet she was glad she had done things properly. Frank had seen that. She had done everything as it should be done.

She went to the table and pulled off the cloth and they stood around, looking down at the plates of food as if uncertain what they were or what should be done with them.

Then Colin took a few steps towards his brother. Frank stood his ground but his eyes were nervous.

'By rights, I should hit you for what you've done,' Colin said, 'and kick you out of this house. You can take it that if it had not been today and her funeral, then that's what I'd have done. You can take it I would.'

He turned and went to the sideboard, opened a bottle of beer and poured it into a glass. Then the others stirred among themselves and May went into the kitchen to put the kettle on and to clear her mind of the shock of seeing him, and to think what to say or do.

On the way to the church in the car following the hearse Berenice had said, 'I wonder if Frank will dare to show his face.'

'Never,' Colin had said. 'He'd never. He doesn't know about it, anyway.'

Nevertheless, they had waited for his footstep, separately wondering and half expecting until the last possible moment. No one had spoken his name again and as the service had continued it had gone from their minds.

He looks the same, May thought. Older but the same. The same face. The same body, no fatter, no thinner, the same watching eyes. The same.

She could not believe that he had dared to come. He had ruined their lives and taken away every friend they had, tainted their memories and left a terrible doubt hanging over their childhood, even though they knew in their hearts that the things he had told were untrue, for those things could not be unsaid and there would always be the suspicion. She prayed that he would simply go so that when she went back into the front room there would be a space and they would move together to fill it and he would never come here again.

But when she carried in the teapot he was standing opposite her, his back to the window, and the sun forming a halo behind his head. She looked directly into his eyes. How can you grow up with someone from birth and know nothing about them, she thought, share parents and brother and sister with them, share a house, rooms, a table, holidays, play, illnesses, games and not know them?

And it flashed through her mind again, as it had done every day since knowing what he had written, that, after all, it might be true and they had chosen to forget but Frank had not forgotten. What then? But it was not true. She knew that as well as she knew her own name and her own self. No word of it was true.

She poured the tea and he came over and took a cup, not looking at her or speaking, and carried it back to the far corner of the room beside the window.

Berenice watched him, then looked at May.

May kept her face blank.

They stood in silence, separated from one another as if they were pieces placed on a board. The cups chinked in the saucers. Frank looked out of the window.

Colin said, 'We should read the will now. It's the right thing to do.'

May had forgotten. It was some time since Bertha had told her that her will was in the small drawer of the bureau. May had gone there that evening, taken out the long cream envelope, turned it over, put it back and never thought of it again until the day after Bertha had died. Colin had asked and she had fetched it from the drawer and given it to him. He was the eldest child. He should decide. 'We'll do it the way it has always been done,' he had said. 'After the funeral. It's what she would expect.'

It was what had happened after John Prime's death. The Beacon and everything in it plus the small amount in the bank had all passed to Bertha, as they had expected.

'We should sit down,' Colin said.

They waited.

He had taken the envelope out of his inner pocket and held it in his hand. He looked at it. Then he took the chair at the head of the table and gestured to May and Berenice. Janet went to the sideboard and picked up the teapot and Joe Jory followed her into the kitchen, closing the door.

'Are you expecting to sit down with us?' Colin asked without looking at his brother.

'I'll stand here.'

'Right.'

They waited and the sun was hot and bright and everything was silent save for the small sounds Colin made as he took his spectacles out of their case, slit open the long envelope and unfolded the paper.

Berenice half closed her eyes against the sun. She wanted to go home so as to be away from Frank and the atmosphere of mistrust and strangeness he had brought into the house, and the will, she knew, would have nothing to do with her, the youngest child and a girl, though perhaps Bertha might have left her the walnut sewing case she had loved as a child. She did not want anything else.

May deliberately suspended all thought, all feeling, in order to get through the rest of the time until they would all have gone and she would be alone here, as she wanted.

Frank looked out of the window at the deserted farmyard and knew that he should not have come. There was nothing here for him. He thought of the airy white spaces of his flat and the absence of any reminder of this place from which he could barely believe now that he had come. He looked at them seated at the table. Colin. May. Berenice. Who were these people?

Suddenly, he was glad that he had written about them and about the Beacon as he had, because it was

146

all true, though not true in the sense of its being the literal truth. The *spirit* of it was true and the spirit was the truth. He felt a burden he had not known he had been carrying roll off his back.

And then he heard Colin's voice. Colin had begun reading before Frank had realised it and so he missed the first lines of their mother's will. But in any case there were not many.

'"To my younger son, Francis Erwin Prime."'

He heard the unfamiliar name. He did not recognise himself.

There was a silence of such depth and intensity that it frightened him.

Colin read again, his voice almost a whisper. '"To my younger son, Francis Erwin Prime."'

The will was dated eleven years previously. Eleven years. Before any of it. Before the book. Whether or not Bertha had known about the book was irrelevant.

Frank looked at their faces.

Berenice was staring, eyes wide, cheeks scarlet, mouth a small puckered little o.

May had her hands together in front of her face but he could see the chalk white of the skin between the long fingers.

Colin had laid down the sheet of paper but kept his hand upon it, his head down as he read again and again.

147

From the kitchen came the crash of china being dropped onto the stone floor, then Janet's little cry, Joe Jory's rumbling voice.

Bertha had left the Beacon to Frank. The house. Its contents. The land. On the understanding that May should be allowed to remain there for the rest of her life. There was a hundred pounds each left to Colin and to Berenice. Nothing else.

Frank was as shocked as they were, perhaps more so, and he felt their shock and bewilderment, their anger and disappointment, like a fire which he could not approach, its heat was so great.

But now, Colin got up and walked out. They heard him call to Janet. Berenice fled after him, her face puckered into tears. May neither moved nor spoke. She hardly seemed to breathe.

He should have spoken. He wanted to say that he would have none of it, that the Beacon was theirs, her home, Colin's farm, and that he washed his hands of everything. If he had done that, if he had said it quickly and clearly and walked out of the door and away, perhaps they might have been able to think better of him in the end, even if they could never understand why he had ruined their lives. If he had.

Instead, the idea that the Beacon was his own, entirely his to do with as he chose, flared up inside him like a spurt of energy, exciting him. Suddenly, he knew what he wanted, what he would do.

Berenice was standing in the open doorway, looking at May. Only at May.

May followed her.

They left, Colin and Janet first, then Berenice and Joe Jory with May in the back of the van, and none of them looked back.

Frank went to the sideboard and poured himself a shot of brandy. The sandwiches were curling at the corners, the glaze on the cake was sweating in the sun.

The sun had slipped round the room so that half of it was in shadow.

He went out to the yard. The swifts were soaring. The sky had a silver sheen.

'May?' His voice sounded strange in the empty yard and her name spoken aloud had no meaning.

He went round the empty buildings and found her, as he knew he would, by the broken gate into the old horse pasture, staring up to the hill.

'What will you do?' May asked at once. 'What will you do now?' Her voice was without expression.

Frank looked slowly around. At the fields baking in the sun. The parched grass. The cracks in the mud around the gate. Back at the house. Until that moment he had had no thought as to the answer. What would he do?

But as they stood there, a yard apart, not looking at one another, with the swallows flying in and out of the empty buildings behind them, he knew. It was not a decision made, it was just knowledge. He knew.

'Come here,' he said.

May did not stir but he sensed the tension in her.

'What is there for you here?' she asked. 'You hate this place. You said so. There was never anything for you here but misery. You said.'

He did not answer. He did not have to.

'When will you come?'

He shrugged. 'I have to sell up in London. After that.'

'Where are you staying now?'

'Nowhere. I didn't bring anything.'

'You'd better stay here then.'

'I'll go back. Ring for a taxi and get the train. There'll be one.'

'Probably.'

'You?'

She looked round. 'Me?' She did not understand.

'What will you do?'

Until that moment, May would have said that she knew her own future well enough. It was here. She had come back to the Beacon all those years ago because she had failed to make another sort of life and she had no thought of trying again. She might have said that her mother had made her stay but that was not the whole truth. Bertha had only had the power that May allowed her.

Frank. If Bertha had known about his book, would she have left him the Beacon? But Bertha had not known. They had done that. They had kept it from her.

'We never told her,' May said now. 'We said nothing. You didn't deserve that, but she did.'

The sun was bright on the far fields now. Behind them, the yard was in shadow.

She could go. Because Bertha had said she could stay here for the rest of her life did not mean that she was obliged to do so. She could go anywhere at all. Where? It was as though she saw the whole world and everything in it in one second, every possibility was set before her. And then a shutter clicked and it was gone.

'I will stay here,' May said.

*

A future with the brother whom she did not know and who had written the terrible things which had ruined their lives and stained their past, spoilt their memories of happiness, such a future was unimaginable.

But Frank returned to London, sold the flat, packed up what he wanted to keep of his possessions, which was little enough when it came down to it. He returned to the Beacon towards the end of that long golden autumn and took over the attic rooms, but left everything else as it was, as it had always been.

Once or twice he said that in the spring they should move out this or decorate that and May supposed that he was right, for the house was shabby and he could make what changes he wanted.

Colin and Berenice never came back to the Beacon. Sometimes, May drove out to the florist's or the cottage, but there was a distance between them now, and it widened and became a strain so that, gradually, they saw one another less and less.

Once, on the first chilly evening when May had lit a fire in the grate, she asked him why he had written what he had, why he had told the lies and named them all as he had done.

'I never understood,' she said. 'I still don't understand.'

'No,' he said.

'Did you do it on purpose, to hurt?'

He was silent. Because he asked himself the question every day and could never properly answer. All he knew was that he had always hated this house and felt a misfit among them, and when he had found a way of paying them back and getting a kind of revenge, he had done so. The money was irrelevant, though he had enjoyed some of the fame. He had always intended to leave a mark deeper and more lasting than the near-invisible writing made by the others.

'Did it make you happy?'

He did not know. But it had given him satisfaction. He had changed the way things were seen and the way they would be remembered. He had changed the way other people thought of them.

The autumn slipped down into one of the harshest winters for years so that they had no time or energy left for argument and scarcely any for conversation. They got through the days as best they could, cut off from the rest of the world by the snow and blizzards, the ice and gales, and later the floods as the thaw came, and it was as though they each lived surrounded by an invisible, impenetrable bubble, almost entirely unaware of one another.

But once or twice, May came upon him standing in the hall and staring at the door of the cupboard under the stairs, and remembered the horrors that had long ago pursued her and did not like to catch his eye.